RANDOM HOUSE
LARGE
PRINT

OBSESSION

ALSO BY STUART WOODS
AVAILABLE FROM RANDOM HOUSE
LARGE PRINT

Near Miss (A Stone Barrington Novel by
Stuart Woods, with Brett Battles)
Distant Thunder
(A Stone Barrington Novel)
Black Dog (A Stone Barrington Novel)
An Extravagant Life
A Safe House (A Stone Barrington Novel)
Criminal Mischief
(A Stone Barrington Novel)
Foul Play (A Stone Barrington Novel)
Class Act (A Stone Barrington Novel)
Jackpot (A Teddy Fay Novel)
Double Jeopardy
(A Stone Barrington Novel)
Hush-Hush (A Stone Barrington Novel)
Shakeup (A Stone Barrington Novel)

OBSESSION

Stuart Woods

AND BRETT BATTLES

RANDOM HOUSE
LARGE PRINT

All rights reserved. Published in the United States of America by Random House Large Print in association with G. P. Putnam's Sons, an imprint of Penguin Random House LLC.

Cover illustration © Mike Heath

The Library of Congress has established a Cataloging-in-Publication record for this title.

ISBN: 978-0-593-74383-6

www.penguinrandomhouse.com/large-print-format-books

FIRST LARGE PRINT EDITION

Printed in the United States of America

1st Printing

OBSESSION

1

TEDDY FAY FLICKED HIS GAZE TO THE REARVIEW mirror and grimaced. The gray sedan was still following him.

Returning his attention to the blacktop ahead, he searched for a turnoff to another road he could use to help him lose his tail. But there wasn't even a wide enough spot where he could pull over. For as far as he could see, the road in front of him was squeezed between the rise of a mountain slope on one side and its descent on the other.

When he glanced again at the mirror, he caught sight of the fear in his own eyes. Fear that this lonely mountain road would be where he died.

He squeezed the steering wheel and shook the

thought away. He couldn't let them win. Would not let them win.

He glanced again at the car in the mirror. "Go ahead. Give me your best shot. I will not let you get to me today."

With renewed determination, he pressed down hard on the gas. For the first time since he'd realized he was being followed, the gap between the other vehicle and his grew instead of shrinking.

If he could, he would have gone even faster, but knew if he did, the force of a turn might send him crashing into the hillside or flying over the drop-off.

He rounded another ridge, hoping this time he'd spot a turnoff he could use to escape, but the twisting road continued as far as he could see.

He swallowed back his fear. "You can do this. You have to. For them."

He leaned toward the steering wheel, his eyes glued to the road ahead just as the other car came into view behind him.

"Cut." Peter Barrington's voice came through a speaker mounted under the dash of Teddy's car. "I think we got it, Mark."

The tension in Teddy's face vanished. "Excellent. If you're happy, I'm happy."

Teddy released the steering wheel and leaned back. His car was being towed behind the camera vehicle that had been filming him, and he'd only been pretending to drive.

Handling the mountain road on his own would have been child's play. But, alas, today he wasn't Teddy Fay, but rather Academy Award–winning actor Mark Weldon, one of his three main identities. The other was that of film producer Billy Barnett.

Thanks to a talent for altering his appearance, honed during years spent in the CIA, only a select few knew that the three men were one and the same.

This trip up the mountain was Teddy's and the crew's fifth of the day. On the first three, a cameraman had been in the seat beside Teddy, filming close-ups and shots of the pursuing sedan. During the last two trips, Peter's crew had been focused on capturing exterior shots. Peter was the film's director, and the only director for whom actor Mark Weldon worked.

The film was called **Storm's Eye.** Its plot centered on a man named Tyler Storm, who'd spent most of his life on the wrong side of the law but was now trying to make amends for his past deeds. Peter had written the part of Storm with Mark in mind, a lead role to celebrate Mark's status as a major award winner.

The camera truck towed Teddy's car into a dirt parking lot where several other production vehicles waited, as well as Peter, who was standing behind the television on which he'd been watching the camera feed.

When Teddy climbed out of the car, he gave Luke Reed, the man in charge of the rig carrying Teddy's sedan, a nod. "Thanks for not driving us off the cliff."

"They have to pay extra for that."

"Then I'm thankful we have a cheap producer."

"Ha, I'll tell Billy you said that when I see him."

"Trust me, it's not anything he doesn't already know." Teddy smiled to himself. If only Luke knew. When Teddy reached Peter, who was reviewing what they had shot, he glanced at the monitor. "Everything look good?"

"See for yourself."

Peter pressed a button and the footage from the last trip up the mountain began to play. Teddy had no ego when it came to his acting. All he wanted to do was a good job. When he watched himself, he did so rationally, looking for how he could improve his performance.

The direct shots of Teddy were full of tension and worry, while the footage of the pursuing sedan had the right sense of urgency he knew Peter was after. As he watched, he picked out a few moments in which he felt he could have done a better job, but he was pleased overall.

Peter smiled as the playback ended. "I'd say you're starting to get the hang of this acting thing."

"Maybe someday I can make a living at it."

"It's always good to have goals, even for you."

With his lead role in **Storm's Eye,** Teddy was making enough from Mark Weldon's acting work to live quite well. Given the even larger amount he earned as Billy Barnett, and the tidy sum he'd already amassed before entering the film business, Teddy was more than comfortable.

"Do we need to go again?" he asked.

Peter clapped him on the back. "I've got what I need. You're wrapped for today. Go back to the hotel. Grab a drink and enjoy some time by the pool."

"I like the way you think."

"Then you'll love this. If I'm not mistaken, you're off tomorrow morning, too."

"You're full of good news today."

Peter chuckled in a not-so-fast kind of way. "I was thinking that if you see Billy, you could tell him tomorrow morning might be a good time for a set visit." Unlike Luke the camera truck driver, Peter knew all about Teddy's identities.

"If I happen to run into him, I'll let him know."

2

TEDDY FELT THE FAMILIAR SENSATION OF BEING watched the moment he stepped into the lobby of the Santa Barbara Hills Hotel.

At least two-thirds of the patrons were sneaking glances at him. Since receiving his Oscar for best supporting actor, Mark Weldon could no longer roam the streets—or in this case, walk through a hotel lobby—unrecognized. It was all rather unfortunate. The persona had served Teddy well when no one had known who Mark was. But gone were the days of conducting any truly covert work as the actor. He had no choice now but to limit Mark's appearances to shoot days like today, and big events at which Mark's attendance was expected.

"Hello, Mark."

Teddy turned toward the familiar voice of Ben Bacchetti, head of Centurion Studios, the studio behind all of Peter Barrington's movies. Like their fathers, Peter and Ben were best friends. Some friendships might be strained by working together, but theirs had only grown stronger.

Ben walked toward Teddy from the direction of the hotel restaurant, in the company of Peter's father, Stone Barrington. A successful lawyer with a reputation for being an expert at handling difficult situations, Stone was on Centurion's board of directors. He was also the man responsible for Teddy working with Ben and Peter.

"Ben, Stone, isn't this a pleasant surprise."

"Good to see you, Mark," Stone said.

"Here to check up on the shoot?"

Ben shook his head. "Not this trip. We're here for a meeting with a production company looking for a studio partner. I'll be heading back to L.A. when we're done."

"Don't production companies typically come to you?"

"This isn't a typical production company. Have you heard of Carl Novak?"

"The tech billionaire?"

"That's the one. You've probably seen his wife before, too. Rebecca Novak? She used to be a model. You name a fashion magazine, and she's been on the cover."

"They want to get into the film business?"

"They already have a few productions underway, documentaries and films that deal with problems that don't get a lot of attention. Without a studio partner like us, they'd be stuck making only a film or two a year. They'd like to do more than that. We're one of several groups they're talking to." Ben's phone buzzed. He checked the screen. "Our car's here. We'll see you later, Mark."

Ben headed for the exit, but Stone turned to Teddy instead of immediately following. "Could you do me a favor?"

Teddy arched an eyebrow. "Depends on the favor."

"If you run into Billy Barnett, can you tell him I'd love to have dinner with him? Say, seven-thirty?"

Teddy twisted his head to the side, attempting to look at his back.

"What are you doing?"

"I'm trying to see if someone put a Billy Barnett's personal assistant sign on my back. He has a secretary and an **actual** personal assistant now, you know. You could call one of them, and they'd let him know."

Stone smiled and patted him on the arm. "I figure this way's faster."

3

ACROSS TOWN, THE OWNER OF SMILING EYES FLOWER
Shop tore off the receipt and held it out. "Thank
you, Mrs. Novak. I'll make sure they're delivered
to your house by one p.m. tomorrow."

"Perfect." Rebecca Novak glanced at the clock
on the wall. It was already a quarter to three. "Is
that the right time?"

The clerk looked to see what she was talking
about and nodded. "Within a minute or two,
I think."

"I didn't realize it was so late. Thank you again
for your help." Rebecca returned her wallet to her
purse and hurried out the door.

She'd spent more time in the shop than
she'd planned and would need to rush to get

home in time for the start of the meeting with Centurion Studios.

As she approached her car, she noticed the passenger door of the sedan beside hers was open, blocking her way. A man was leaning into the other vehicle, as if he was getting something out of the glove compartment.

At any other time, she would have patiently waited for him to finish, but she was already running behind. "Excuse me."

The man didn't seem to hear her.

"Sir? If you don't mind, I need to get into my car."

He looked over his shoulder and then at her car, as if only now realizing he was in her way. "Oh. I am so sorry."

He closed his door and stepped to the side to clear the path.

Once he was out of the way, she flashed him a smile and moved past him. "Thank you."

As she reached for the handle of her door, she sensed a sudden presence behind her, then felt something hard jab into her ribs. Startled, she looked down and saw the muzzle of a gun pressing against her.

"If you do anything to call attention to us, I will kill you."

She stared at him, wide-eyed, then started to pull her purse from her shoulder. "Whatever cash I have, it's yours."

He shoved the gun harder against her side. "You only speak when I ask a question. Otherwise, you remain silent. Nod if you understand."

"What?"

He ground his gun into her again. "Understand?"

She squeezed her lips together and nodded.

"Good. Take a step back and open the door to my car."

Her eyes widened. But before he could twist the gun into her again, she did as he'd asked.

"Now, get in."

When she didn't move right away, he said, "I can either kill you here or take you with me. Either way the message will be sent. The choice is yours."

She hesitated another second before ducking down and climbing into the seat. The instant she was inside, someone who'd been hiding in the back grabbed her arms. She tried to struggle free, but a wet cloth flopped over her mouth and nose. Rebecca twisted her head back and forth to get out from under it, but a hand held it in place.

Her head began spinning as a wave of vertigo washed over her. She tried to fight it, but with every breath she took she felt her consciousness slipping further away.

Though she heard her captors speaking, their voices were muted by the thick cloud of confusion churning in her head, and it took her a second to realize they weren't speaking in English. Yet she still found she understood a word or two here and there.

"Get her key," one of the voices said.

She felt her purse being tugged from her shoulder, but she could do nothing about it. Around her, the world grew dark as her vision narrowed.

"That's right, Mrs. Novak. Go to sleep."

As the last of her consciousness began to fade away, she realized why the language sounded so familiar.

They were speaking in her husband's native Croatian.

ZORAN JANIC TRIED VERY HARD NOT TO GLANCE AT his phone. His cousin, Neno Bilic, was supposed to have contacted him an hour ago. If something had gone wrong with the operation, Janic would not be pleased.

Two weeks ago, he had sent Neno, along with two of Janic's other men, Sava Kordo and Pavel Dodic, to America to deal with a problem Janic had neglected for too long. Fourteen days should have been more than enough time to rattle the Novaks in preparation for the main event. Which, if things had gone well, should have begun within the last couple of hours.

Janic walked to his window, his jaw tense.

Those nosy documentary filmmakers were irritating enough. After they had shown up in Croatia and started digging up information on crime networks in the Balkans, networks that with just enough poking would lead right to him, he found an easy enough way to shut down production. But his plans changed to something bigger when he learned Carl Novak and his wife, Rebecca, were the ones backing the film.

It was a sign that the time for payback had arrived, a sign Janic had been waiting years for.

Finally, his phone rang.

"Yes?"

"It's me," Neno said. "We have her."

All the tension Janic had been holding on to vanished. "Any problems?"

"None."

"No one saw you?"

"No one."

"Good work. Proceed as planned."

Janic ended the call, grabbed the bottle of whiskey off the shelf behind him, and poured himself a celebratory drink.

4

CARL AND REBECCA NOVAK'S MANSION SAT ON FIVE acres in the foothills on the north side of Santa Barbara, hidden behind a high wall.

When Stone and Ben arrived, they were met at their car by a smartly dressed man, who looked to be in his forties.

"Mr. Bacchetti, Mr. Barrington, I'm Andrew Vulin, Mr. and Mrs. Novak's estate manager." The man spoke with a European accent. "If you would follow me."

The grand entry to the house featured dueling staircases and a gorgeous chandelier that hovered over the center of the space.

Vulin led them down a Spanish-tiled hallway on the first floor, lined with original illustrations hanging on the walls. They passed several rooms before stopping in front of a closed set of double doors. Vulin knocked twice, then opened both doors and announced, "Centurion Studios." He moved out of the way and nodded for Stone and Ben to enter.

The high-ceilinged room was surrounded by bookcases that covered almost every available inch of wall space. In the center were a pair of leather sofas facing each other, separated by a coffee table.

Standing near the sofas were two men. One was unmistakably Carl Novak. A week seldom went by when his image didn't appear either in print or on TV. More often than not, he would be in the company of his wife, Rebecca.

Stone and Ben had been told she would be at the meeting, too, but the only other person in the room was an older gentleman standing with Novak.

Novak glanced past Stone and Ben at the doors as they closed, as if expecting someone else to enter. When his attention returned to his guests, he took a step forward.

"Thank you for coming. I'm Carl Novak." His native Croatian accent was subtle, as if he'd worked hard to rid himself of it.

"Ben Bacchetti. Thanks for inviting us."

"Stone Barrington."

Novak shook hands with them, then motioned at the other man. "This is our counsel, Richard Mori."

Another round of handshakes ensued.

"We appreciate your coming all the way out here," the lawyer said. "Carl and Rebecca both thought this would be a more comfortable setting than my stuffy office."

"It's a gorgeous house," Ben said.

Novak smiled. "Thank you."

Mori motioned to the sofas. "Shall we sit?"

Ben and Stone sat on one sofa, Novak and his lawyer on the other.

Mori appeared to be waiting for Novak to start speaking, but his client was looking at his watch, lost in thought.

"Carl?"

Novak blinked at the sound, then chuckled self-consciously. "My apologies, gentlemen. I was expecting my wife to be here. She explains everything much better than I do." He smiled. "As you are aware, the goal of our production company is to make films that will inspire viewers. What we don't want to do is turn out mindless movies only meant to make money. No offense intended."

Ben shook his head. "None taken. We try not to do that also."

"I believe that. Your list of quality films is remarkable. That's why we made sure you would be one of the studios we met with."

"We appreciate that."

It was clear Novak was still distracted, but as he described his and his wife's plans for their company in more detail, he began to settle into himself. And by the time he summed things up, all traces of his previous preoccupation had disappeared.

"We know that focusing on topics of inequality and highlighting problems such as crime and poverty and other basic inequities of life isn't always an easy sell. But we believe that by bringing awareness to topics such as these, through well-made stories and documentaries, we will find an eager audience. And we hope our films will inspire some viewers into action."

"That's a refreshing change from many of the production companies we've met with over the years," Ben said. "While I'm not going to lie and say profits aren't important, we at Centurion Studios believe there should always be room for the kind of work you're doing." He took in both Novak and Mori. "We may not be the largest studio in Hollywood, but we feel our unmatched commitment to quality entertainment makes us the perfect fit for your plans."

"Your recent successes at the Academy Awards speaks to your commitment. Rebecca and I were very impressed."

The talk turned to the more concrete ways they could help each other, and how a partnership between them might work.

When all had been said, and questions asked and answered, Novak said, "Thank you, gentlemen. You have more than lived up to my expectations. I only regret Rebecca couldn't be here. I know she wanted to be."

"We look forward to meeting her in the future. If either of you would like to talk more, please don't hesitate to call."

They said their goodbyes, and Mori escorted Stone and Ben back through the house.

When they reached the front door, Mori said, "We still have a few other meetings set up. It could be a week or two before we make our decision. But I will say, Carl wasn't lying when he said he was impressed."

Ben held out his hand and they shook. "Whoever you go with, I'm sure it will be the right choice."

"Thank you."

Mori opened the door, and Ben walked outside.

Before Stone could follow, Mori touched his arm. "Mr. Barrington, I'm wondering if you might have a little time. There's a matter I'd like to discuss with you."

"I'll be in town until tomorrow evening. When would you like to meet?"

"How about now?"

5

"MIND IF I JOIN YOU?"

Teddy looked up from his poolside table at a smiling Tessa Tweed Bacchetti. "I'd be insulted if you didn't."

She took the chair next to his, then nodded at the script in his hand. "Memorizing your lines? Shouldn't you know them by now?"

"This isn't **Storm's Eye.** It's a draft of Peter's next picture."

Her expression brightened in genuine interest. Like Mark Weldon, Tessa was an Academy Award–winning actor and they had appeared in several pictures together. She was playing Tyler Storm's niece in **Storm's Eye.**

"Don't worry," Teddy said. "There's a part for you."

She scrunched up her mouth. "I wasn't even thinking about that."

He raised an eyebrow. "You weren't?"

"Well, maybe a little." She shot a look at the script. "Is it a good part?"

He moved it to his other side, out of her reach. "Now, now. You know Peter wouldn't want me to say anything."

"You can at least tell me if the script is good."

"When have you read one of Peter's scripts that wasn't?"

"True."

A pool attendant approached their table. "May I get you anything, Ms. Tweed?"

"A sparkling water, thank you." When the man left, she turned back to Teddy. "Can you at least tell me the title?"

"It's not final."

"This is Hollywood. Nothing is ever final until a picture is in the theaters."

"Okay, fine." He set the script on the table.

Tessa leaned forward and read the title page aloud. **"The Zurich Affair."** She looked at Teddy, excited. "We're going to shoot in Europe?"

"Unless Billy Barnett can talk him out of it."

"He'd better not. And you can tell him I said that." Tessa was also a member of the exclusive club in on Teddy's secrets.

"I'm sure he's well aware of your feelings."

"There's being well aware of my feelings, and

then there's agreeing with me." She paused in thought. "Maybe I should discuss it with Ben. I'm sure he would support me and can outvote Billy." Ben Bacchetti was not only her husband and the head of Centurion Studios, but also Billy Barnett's boss.

"I was wondering how long until you played that card."

She gasped dramatically and put a hand to her chest. "Whatever do you mean?"

The attendant showed up with Tessa's drink and set it on the table.

"Thank you."

"My pleasure, Ms. Tweed. If you need anything else, let me know."

After they were alone again, Teddy leaned back in his chair and opened the script to the page where he'd left off. "Now, if you don't mind, I'd like to find out what happens to the heroine."

"Heroine?"

Teddy mimed zipping his lips closed.

"Fine." Tessa took a sip of her drink. "I was thinking about going to the spa for a massage anyway."

"That sounds like a plan."

"You really aren't going to let me look at it?"

"I'm really not."

She leaned toward him, and in a quieter voice said, "In all seriousness, how good is it?"

"Honestly, I think it might be Peter's best."

"Now I really need to read it."

"Didn't you say something about a massage?"

She laughed. "All right, all right. I get the hint." She grabbed her glass and stood. "Enjoy the read. Dinner tonight?"

"So you can continue to try convincing me?"

"I would never."

"I'm sure you wouldn't. Unfortunately, I already have plans."

"It was worth a try."

TEDDY RETURNED TO HIS SUITE BY EARLY EVENING and changed from Mark Weldon the actor into Billy Barnett the producer, with the assistance of his makeup kit. He was staying in a suite registered to the latter, as was his preference. A few doors down the hall was a smaller suite in Mark's name. It was for appearances' sake only, so no one would wonder where Mark was staying.

To avoid risking confusion about who was entering whose room, Peter and Tessa were the only other members of the cast or crew who had rooms on Teddy's floor.

When Teddy's transformation was complete, he headed down to the hotel lobby to meet Stone for dinner. But he had taken only a few steps out of the elevator when Stacy Lange intercepted him.

"I thought you weren't coming back until next week."

"Good to see you, too, Stacy."

"Sorry. Nice to see you, Mr. Barnett."

A former Centurion Studios production assistant, Stacy had been promoted to the position of Billy Barnett's personal assistant. Teddy had not been keen on the idea, but Peter and Ben had insisted.

"Mark Weldon is spending more time in front of the camera, which means Billy is on set a lot less," Ben had said. "Stacy will be Billy's eyes and ears. Plus, if anyone is looking for him, they'll have someone to talk to."

She'd been at the job for two months now, and Teddy had to admit her involvement helped.

"Had a change of plans," he told her. "How's the shoot going?"

"Good. We're on schedule and Peter says he's happy with the footage."

"And what do you say?"

"That he's right. Everything looks great. Mark is doing a wonderful job. I think he might even get another nomination."

"Did Mark pay you to tell me that?"

"I'm serious. He's wonderful."

"Do me a favor. Don't let him know."

"Why not?"

He leaned toward her and whispered, "Best to keep his ego in check."

She laughed. "My lips are sealed."

"That's what makes you the perfect assistant."

She beamed. "I have dinner plans this evening, but if you need me to give you a more detailed briefing now, I could change my schedule."

"I'll be on set tomorrow morning," Teddy said. "Let's do it then. Unless there's an emergency we need to discuss now?"

She looked relieved. "No emergencies."

"Then I'll see you in the morning."

As she walked away, Stone joined Teddy. "If it isn't the elusive Billy Barnett."

"In the flesh. Is it just the two of us?"

"Peter's meeting us at the restaurant in an hour. You and I have a stop to make first. You don't mind driving, do you?"

They retrieved Teddy's car from the valet and headed out. Usually, Teddy drove rental cars when on location, but since Santa Barbara was only a couple hours northwest of Los Angeles, he'd driven up in his classic 1958 Porsche 356 Speedster.

"What's this stop we have to make?" Teddy asked as he drove Stone through the city.

"I met with someone today who may be in need of help from our mutual acquaintance."

"Acting lessons from Mark Weldon?"

Stone smirked. "Your other friend."

Of course, he meant Teddy Fay, the not-as-dead-as-most-people-thought-he-was former CIA operative.

Teddy wanted to ask more but remained silent. The Porsche's top was down, and while it was unlikely someone could overhear them, the possibility did exist.

With Stone offering directions, they made their way to a four-story building in the downtown business district. On the top floor, they entered the law firm of Mori & Jenkins.

Stone approached the receptionist. "Stone Barrington to see Richard Mori."

Mori entered the lobby less than half a minute later, appearing considerably more tense than he'd been that afternoon.

Stone motioned to Teddy. "This is Billy Barnett. Billy, Richard Mori."

Mori shook Teddy's hand. "Thank you for coming. This way, gentlemen."

He led them to his corner office. Stone was surprised to find Carl Novak waiting inside. He had been under the impression that he and Teddy would be meeting with Mori alone.

Novak, who'd been pacing by the windows, stopped the moment they stepped inside. "Oh, thank God."

Teddy glanced at Stone, silently asking what was going on.

Before Stone could answer, Mori said, "There's something you need to see." He circled behind his desk and angled his computer toward the others. On the screen was a paused video. "The situation has changed."

He clicked the PLAY button.

The image was a static shot of a windowless, concrete room. Pushed against the wall was a cot, on which lay a woman, either asleep or unconscious. Taped to the wall behind her was a piece of paper with a large number five written on it.

A digitally altered voice then came out of the speaker. "Mr. Novak, if you would like your wife returned unharmed, do not contact the police or any other agency. Do not talk to the press. If you contact any of them, we will find out and we will kill her. You will then spend the rest of your life knowing your inability to follow instructions caused her demise. The time to pay for your mistakes has come. We will be in touch."

The screen went black.

Teddy looked first at Mori and then at Novak. It wasn't hard to put together the pieces of what was happening. "I take it the woman on the bed is your wife?"

Novak nodded. "Yes. Rebecca."

"When was the last time you saw her?"

"Right after lunch. She went out to run a few

errands. She was supposed to be home for our meeting with Centurion Studios, but as Stone knows, she didn't make it. I—I thought she was running late. But . . ."

"Have you called the police or the FBI?"

Novak looked shocked at the suggestion. "You heard them. If I do that, they'll kill her."

Teddy turned back to Stone and Mori. "Is this connected to what we were originally going to discuss?"

"Of course it is," Novak snapped, answering for them. "What else could it be?"

"I have no idea. Could have been a pitch to sell me a time-share, for all I know. If it's not asking too much, maybe someone can bring me up to speed."

Novak glared at Mori. "This is a waste of time." He waved an angry hand at the computer. "They're threatening to kill her. How can an East Coast lawyer and a film producer help us? We need someone who can—"

"Carl, please." Mori's voice was calm and controlled. "Stone has considerable experience dealing with this sort of matter. And Mr. Barnett—"

"Knows someone who can handle this for you," Stone finished. "Quietly."

"That's if someone tells me what's going on," Teddy said. "**And** my friend agrees to help."

Novak grimaced, then sighed. "Fine. Tell him."

Mori motioned to the chairs on the other side of his desk. "Please, sit."

Stone and Teddy did so, while Novak remained on his feet.

"As I explained to Stone this afternoon, over the past few weeks, someone has been stealing objects from the Novaks' home and leaving threatening messages in their place. There have also been other disturbances, like cars being tampered with and the driveway gate being jammed multiple times."

Teddy leaned forward. "Are the notes only threats or are there demands, too?"

Mori grabbed a folder off his desk and handed it to Teddy. Inside were half a dozen pieces of paper, each with a typed message printed on it. Teddy flipped through them. Most were variations of empty threats: **It's your turn** or **There's nothing you can do to stop us.** The one that stood out most to Teddy read: **Time to pay for your mistakes.** Those same words had been spoken on the video.

Mori looked at Teddy. "Stone told me your friend has experience with delicate situations. Has he ever handled a kidnapping before?"

"More than once."

"Do you think he can help us?"

Teddy closed the folder. "I won't know until I ask him."

Novak shook his head, exasperated. "We don't have time to—"

Teddy held up a hand, cutting him off. "What I can say is that I'll have an answer within the hour. Will that work?"

"It will," Mori said. Novak looked like he wanted to argue further, but he held his tongue.

To Novak, Teddy said, "If he does agree to get involved, he'll likely want to send someone to search your house, in case whoever has been leaving you the notes has also left clues behind. That won't be a problem, will it?"

Novak shook his head. "Of course not. Whatever will help."

"Best not to let your staff know what's really going on, though. Pretend you're considering changing security companies, and the people who show up are there to do an assessment."

"I'll let Mr. Vulin know someone is coming. He's the estate manager. Your friend can contact him directly to coordinate."

"Again, this is **if** my friend decides he can help."

"Please do whatever you can to persuade him."

After getting a list of employees who worked at the estate and Novak's and Mori's direct contact info, Teddy and Stone left the office.

When they reached the Porsche, Teddy said, "Not exactly the way I was expecting my evening to go."

"If it's any consolation, I wasn't expecting his wife to be kidnapped this afternoon, either. But if anyone can find her, it's you."

"Thanks for the vote of confidence."

"You are going to help them, right?"

"I'll do what I can."

"Thank you. If you need any assistance from me, let me know."

"Don't worry. You're at the top of my list."

6

EARLIER THAT EVENING, MATTHEW WAGNER SAT IN
the driver's seat of his car, looking through
his binoculars.

The crowd of fans at the entrance to the Santa
Barbara Hills Hotel driveway was the same size
as it had been the past few evenings. Its members
held magazines and notebooks and photographs,
prepared to grab an autograph if the opportunity
arose. A majority also had phones at the ready.
Every time someone stepped out of the hotel,
dozens of pictures were snapped—in case the
person was one of the stars of **Storm's Eye.**

A pair of rent-a-cops made sure the onlookers
stayed on the sidewalk and off hotel property.
What they couldn't stop was the shouts that

rang out from the crowd whenever the hotel door opened.

The group was filled with amateurs, as far as Matthew was concerned. If they really wanted autographs or pictures, all they needed to do was enter the hotel as if they had rooms there and walk around.

Matthew had been inside the hotel multiple times since the cast had arrived. He'd seen several of the actors lounging at the pool, eating at the restaurant, and drinking at the bar. Mark Weldon had even walked by him once. The only star Matthew hadn't seen yet was the only one who mattered to him.

Two men exited the hotel to calls from the fans and climbed into a classic convertible Porsche. Matthew recognized one as Billy Barnett, producer of **Storm's Eye.** The other man was director Peter Barrington's father, Stone Barrington, a board member of Centurion Studios.

On one of Matthew's bedroom walls back in L.A., he'd taped photographs of anyone associated with Centurion Studios so that he could recognize them by sight. Some images had been clipped from magazines, and some he'd taken himself. Under each was a label identifying the people in the shot, written in Matthew's precise, error-free script.

He watched the two men drive away, then

promptly forgot about them. Barnett and Barrington were of little interest to him.

More people came and went from the hotel, but none were who Matthew wanted to see.

He could feel his annoyance growing. This would be the third night in a row he'd sat there without seeing her. He was getting tired of waiting. Maybe it was time to try something more direct.

He was about to lower the binoculars and call it a night when the hotel entrance opened again, and Tessa Tweed walked out, sweeping away all his anger and frustration in an instant.

Tessa was the female lead of **Storm's Eye.** In Matthew's opinion, she was the best actress to ever grace the screen. She could do drama or comedy or action or anything she wanted. And it didn't hurt that she was beautiful, too.

Accompanying Tessa were Logan Chase and Adriene Adele, two other actors in the movie, and another woman Matthew had seen on set but didn't know her name. Not an actor, but a crew member of some kind.

The four of them waited until a valet drove up in a blue BMW. Chase's car, Matthew knew. Just like he knew the vehicles driven by everyone important in the cast and crew.

As they climbed into the sedan, Matthew lowered the binoculars and started his car.

7

TESSA PUT A COMFORTING HAND ON ADRIENE'S shoulder. "I wouldn't worry. If Peter had a problem with the scene, he would have said something."

The two of them, along with Stacy and Logan, were eating dinner at a small Thai restaurant in downtown Santa Barbara.

Adriene smiled weakly and stabbed a fork at her food. "I guess. I just feel like I wasn't at my best today."

"Look, if it's still bothering you tomorrow, talk to him."

"I wouldn't want to waste his time."

This was Adriene's first time working for Peter and only her fourth film ever. Peter had cast her in a much larger role than any of her previous parts. It was natural that she felt nervous.

"You wouldn't be," Stacy said. "He's easy to talk to. I'm sure he'd rather you let him know that something was bothering you than if you didn't."

Tessa could see Adriene still wasn't convinced. "How about this? We can talk to him together. I'll tell him I wasn't sure about the scene I did and ask him if it turned out okay. That should make it easier for you to bring up your concerns."

"No, I don't want to drag you into this."

"You wouldn't be. I'm offering."

Adriene bit her lower lip. "Are you sure?"

"I wouldn't have suggested it if I wasn't."

Adriene finally allowed herself to smile. "That would be great. Thank you. I owe you big time."

"You can pay me back by doing the same for someone else once you become a big star."

"If that happens, I will."

"Not if. **When.**"

Logan rested a forearm on the table and leaned forward, a smirk on his face. "When I was starting out, I questioned everything I did."

One of Tessa's eyebrows shot up. "You can remember that far back?"

Stacy snorted and quickly covered her mouth. "Sorry."

He gave them each a dramatic scowl, then continued as if Tessa hadn't spoken. "There was this one picture, **The Swedish Ambassador.** You must have seen it. Everyone did. I played . . ."

Tessa tuned him out. Logan was nice, and a

fine actor, but the man had yet to meet a topic of conversation he couldn't make about himself.

She let her gaze drift across the room.

The restaurant had five tables and four booths, all currently occupied. Not surprising, given how delicious the food was.

Tessa caught several of the other diners glancing at her table and then away again. She should be used to the attention by now, but it still caught her by surprise. The price of fame, as they say.

The only diner not interested in her and her companions was a man sitting alone by the window, reading a book while he ate.

She watched him for a moment, wondering what the book's title was, then turned back to her friends.

Unsurprisingly, Logan was still talking.

"It's not every day a star like Todd Norman compliments you. He even said there'd be a part for me in any movie he was in, if I wanted it."

"Have you taken him up on that?" Adriene asked.

"Not yet. I like to spread my wings. Work with different people. It gives me more options."

"I guess that makes sense."

Tessa laughed. "He's lying. If Todd Norman called and said he had a role for him in his next picture, Logan would snap it up without even asking how many lines he'd have."

Logan looked as if he were going to protest,

but then he shrugged. "Well, yeah. I mean, he **is** Todd Norman."

They all had a good laugh, and the conversation switched to topics less Logan focused.

When they'd finished their food, Stacy checked the time. "I should head back."

"Me, too," Tessa said.

Logan looked disappointed. "No drinks first? I heard about this cool bar not far from here."

"We all have early calls tomorrow."

"It's not even ten yet. I only want to have a little more fun before we go back."

"And we want to be well rested before we work in the morning. Which might be why I'm playing the lead, Adriene will be a star after this picture comes out, and Stacy will soon be producing all our films. While you will continue waiting for Todd Norman to call."

"I feel like I should be outraged," Logan said with a laugh.

"Nonsense. This is another story you can tell. The time you were rejected by three beautiful women at once."

8

MATTHEW KEPT TABS ON TESSA AND HER COLLEAGUES out of the corner of his eye as he pretended to read his book. Watching people this way was a skill he'd developed when he was young. It was how he'd kept watch on the jerks who'd liked beating him up in school.

The one time he almost glanced up was when Tessa's gaze fell on him. The desire to look into her eyes was so strong that the only way he stopped himself from turning was to jam his fingernails into his palm.

He'd known before entering the restaurant that getting this close to her would be risky, but he'd been so sure he could do it without being noticed that he ignored his own warning.

He should have listened. He should have

stayed in his car and waited for them to leave. But he had foolishly given in to the temptation. Hopefully, she wouldn't remember him when she saw him again. Because she would see him again. He hadn't come to Santa Barbara only to watch her from a distance.

Soon, they would be eating meals together instead of at separate tables. But tonight, he needed to make himself scarce so as not to jeopardize his plans.

He flagged down the waitress, paid his bill, and left.

By the time Tessa and her friends climbed back into Logan Chase's BMW, Matthew was ready and waiting to follow them again.

9

TEDDY HANDED HIS KEYS TO THE VALET. "KEEP IT
close. I won't be long."

"Yes, sir."

After leaving Mori's office, Teddy and Stone
had headed to Canavo's Ristorante Italiano to
meet Peter. As they entered the restaurant, neither of them noticed the man sitting in a car
across the street, watching them.

A hostess led them to a private dining room
where Peter was already waiting. "I'll let your
waiter know that you've all arrived."

Before she could exit, Teddy said, "Please tell
him to give us fifteen minutes."

She acknowledged his request with a tilt of her
head and closed the door on her way out.

"I was beginning to think I'd be eating by

myself." Peter's grin faltered as he took in his father and Teddy. "You two have that look."

Stone sat down across from his son. "What look?"

"The one you always get when you have something to tell me that I'm not going to like."

"It's hard to get anything by you Barringtons, isn't it?" Teddy said as he pulled out his phone. "Before we ruin your night, Peter, I need to make a call."

As he moved to a corner of the room, he tapped the number for Mike Freeman, CEO of Strategic Services, one of the largest security firms in the country.

Freeman answered on the first ring. "Who do I have the pleasure of speaking with this evening?" He also knew about Teddy's secrets.

"The original edition."

"So not a social call, then."

"When have I **ever** called you to just say hello?"

"Good point. What can I do for you?"

"To start, I need a couple of your men and a security company van here in Santa Barbara tomorrow morning."

"Trouble?"

"You might say that."

"Problems with security at the shoot?" Strategic Services often provided the security for Centurion Studios. In the case of **Storm's Eye,** however, at the request of the Santa Barbara city government, Freeman had subcontracted a local company to handle the job.

"No. Not the shoot."

"Then what?"

"I'd rather not say right now. But I promise to loop you in if it becomes necessary."

"Understood. What time in the morning?"

"Nine a.m.?"

"I can make that happen."

"When you die, I'll have **Not only smart but also reliable** chiseled onto your tombstone."

"Your interest in my legacy is both creepy and appreciated."

"What are friends for? Send me the contact info for your men and I'll let them know where to meet me."

"I'll see to it."

"Thanks, Mike."

"Wait. You said 'to start.' I assume that means there's something else?"

"There is. I'm going to send you a list of people who work at the residence of Carl and Rebecca Novak."

"The billionaire?"

"And his wife. I need background checks on all of them."

"Anything else?"

"That should do it for now."

Instead of joining Stone and Peter at the table after he hung up, Teddy remained standing.

Peter's gaze switched back and forth between him and Stone. "Why do I get the feeling you're about to tell me my lead actor won't be as available as he should be?"

"A woman's been kidnapped," Stone said.

Peter's annoyance vanished. "Who? Wait. Do you mean Rebecca Novak? Does this have anything to do with your meeting from earlier?"

His father nodded. "I know I don't need to say this, but please keep it to yourself."

"Of course." Peter looked at Teddy. "You're going to find her?"

"That's the plan. I'll try not to screw up the schedule too much. But time is everything in situations like this, so it will be helpful if over the next several days you need me less than more."

Peter nodded. "Do what you need to do. I'll move things around."

10

BEFORE DRIVING AWAY FROM THE RESTAURANT, Teddy called Mori. "Is Mr. Novak still with you?"

"He is."

"Can you put me on speaker?"

The line clicked, then Mori said, "We're both listening."

"My friend is available and will start right away."

"Thank you," Novak said, not hiding his relief. "That is excellent news."

"He had a few questions he wanted me to ask."

"Go ahead."

"What kind of car was Rebecca driving this afternoon?"

"A Mercedes-Maybach S 580. It's dark gray."

"License number?"

"I don't have it memorized."

"I have it in our files," Mori said. "I'll text it to you."

"Thanks," Teddy said. "He also wants to know what errands she was running and the route she took, if you happen to know it."

"I know she was dropping some stuff off at the local hospital," Novak said. "We sponsor a program that helps families in need and Rebecca likes to be personally involved. After that, I'm not certain. I believe she said she was stopping by the wine shop."

"Which wine shop?"

"Christine's Fine Wines. It's the only place we use. I think she was also going to the flower shop she loves. What's it called?"

Teddy heard soft tapping coming over the line.

After another moment, Novak said, "Here it is. Smiling Eyes Flower Shop. I can text you all the addresses."

"Great. As soon as possible. Is that it? She didn't go anywhere else?"

"She could have, but those were the only places she mentioned."

"All right. I'll pass the information on."

"Please also give my thanks to . . . I'm sorry, I don't think you told us the name of your friend."

"You're right. I didn't. He prefers it that way."

"I see. I guess that makes sense. Please tell him thank you for agreeing to help."

"Will do. I'll call you if he has any other questions."

Teddy received two texts as he pulled out of the restaurant parking lot. The first was from Mori with the license number for the Mercedes, and the second from Novak containing the addresses.

Teddy headed to the hospital first, hoping Rebecca's Mercedes was there. But it wasn't in any of the nearby lots.

He drove by the wine shop next. It had its own parking area in front of the building, but again, no Maybach.

As he headed toward the flower shop, he checked his rearview mirror. On the trip between the hospital and Christine's Fine Wines, he had noticed a car a half block back, maintaining a constant distance between them. He had thought it a coincidence at the time, but the car was behind him again.

Not a coincidence, after all.

Keeping his speed down so as not to tip the other driver off, Teddy turned at the next road, then turned again two blocks down.

SAVA KORDO EASED HIS SEDAN AROUND THE CORNER and spotted the taillights of the Porsche, right where he expected them to be.

That afternoon, after he and Neno had kidnapped Rebecca Novak, Kordo had followed Neno, who was driving the woman's Mercedes, to a neighborhood far from where they'd taken her. There, they'd ditched her car, then transported her to their hideout and transferred her into their makeshift holding cell. Kordo had then returned to the Novaks' neighborhood, and parked on a street that overlooked their estate. From his observation point, he kept watch on the house.

Thirty minutes after Kordo arrived, a man left the house and climbed into the back seat of a car. The vehicle remained where it was until another man exited the mansion and hopped into the back seat on the other side.

A short time later, the Novaks' lawyer left. Things quieted down after that. Over the next two hours, the only people Kordo saw were a gardener trimming some hedges and a man sweeping the driveway.

When his phone alarm went off at 6:07 p.m., Kordo perked up. That was the time the video of Novak's wife was to be delivered. He was sure he'd see some action then, and he wasn't wrong. Novak had rushed out of his house only a few minutes later and sped away in one of his cars. Kordo had followed him to the lawyer's office.

A half hour after he'd begun keeping watch on the office building, two men arrived in an old

Porsche. Kordo recognized the older of the pair as one of the men he'd seen leave Novak's house that afternoon. The driver of the Porsche was unfamiliar to him, but he had no doubt the pair were there to see Novak and Mori.

They stayed inside the office for less than twenty minutes. When they reappeared, Kordo pointed a directional microphone at them in time to pick up the man he'd recognized from earlier saying, "If anyone can find her, it's you."

Kordo and Neno had predicted that Novak would reach out for help. It was why he'd been keeping a close eye on Novak all day. Good thing, because it looked like they were right to be concerned.

These two didn't look like FBI or local law enforcement, though.

Kordo kept the mic aimed at them as they climbed into the Porsche, but neither said anything more.

He had planned on continuing to trail Novak the rest of the evening, but given what he'd overheard, the two men seemed a more immediate threat.

He followed them to an Italian restaurant. The man who was going to "find her" stayed for only a short time before leaving again.

If Kordo had any doubt the Porsche driver was trying to rescue Rebecca Novak, it vanished as soon as he realized the guy was retracing a part of the route Rebecca had taken that afternoon.

At least he had been until he took an un-expected turn into a residential area and then another a couple of blocks down.

Curious, Kordo continued his pursuit.

11

FOR A MOMENT, THE ROAD BEHIND TEDDY REMAINED
dark. Then like clockwork, the lights of the other
sedan came around the corner.

No question about it. He was being followed.

This was not the first time he'd been in this
position, so he wasn't concerned. In fact, he was
feeling quite the opposite. It seemed a fair bet
that whoever was following him had something
to do with Rebecca's disappearance.

If Teddy could turn the tables on his new
friend, he might be able to wrap this whole thing
up before the night was over.

When he took another turn, he immediately
doused his lights and pulled into the empty
driveway of a dark house. He yanked up on the

emergency brake, killed his engine, and ducked low so that the car looked unoccupied.

WHEN THE PORSCHE TURNED AGAIN, KORDO BEGAN feeling uneasy. Before, the car had been following Rebecca's route, but the last few turns had been a deviation that felt far too strategic.

He'd been working as one of Janic's enforcers for years. And before that, he had grown up as war had ravaged the Balkans. The combined experiences had taught him long ago to listen to his instincts.

And his instincts were telling him to get out of there.

Instead of following the Porsche, he turned down a block early and sped away in the other direction.

TEDDY COUNTED OFF THE SECONDS UNTIL THE SEDAN should have driven passed his hiding place. When it didn't appear, he rose high enough to look over the back of the Porsche.

The street was deserted.

He waited another three minutes in case the sedan had been driving slowly, but the other car didn't show up.

His tail must have realized Teddy had spotted him.

Teddy backed out of the driveway and searched the neighborhood for the sedan, but it was nowhere to be found.

Part of him wanted to keep hunting for it, but Teddy knew he had another critical task to complete tonight. When he had come to Santa Barbara for the **Storm's Eye** shoot, he had expected to be on set most days. He'd planned to spend any time off either relaxing at the hotel or taking drives up the coast. Which was why he had arrived with little more than his car and a suitcase full of clothes. And his makeup kit, of course. He never went anywhere without that.

What he hadn't brought along was anything that would help him solve a kidnapping. That was a problem that needed to be fixed.

So Teddy put the search for Rebecca's car on hold and headed to the freeway.

Once he was driving south on the 101 toward L.A., he called his hacker friend Kevin Cushman, known in certain online circles as Warplord924.

Kevin answered with a distracted "Yes?" In the background, Teddy could hear fighting sound effects from whatever video game Kevin was playing.

Kevin made a very nice living from the comfort of his childhood bedroom, dealing with computer-related issues his clients didn't know how to fix. This also allowed him plenty of time to get lost in the worlds of monsters and aliens and zombies.

"Did I catch you at a bad time?"

"Oh. It's you. Uh, hi. Give me a second." Over the line came clashes of steel and agitated grunts. Teddy was pretty sure several of the latter were not part of the game's soundtrack.

A loud explosion soon drowned out all other sound. As it died away, triumphant music began playing.

"Sorry. Had to beat down some annoying raiders. What's up?"

"I have a project for you."

"Does it involve doing anything illegal?"

"Kevin, I'm shocked. Do you think I would ask you to do something that could get you in trouble?"

"Every time."

"Good. We understand each other. I'm looking for a woman—"

"I feel your pain. But I would rather not get involved in your dating life."

"No offense, but if I needed help in that area, you would be the last person I'd talk to."

"I can respect that."

"The woman I'm looking for has been kidnapped. I need you to check footage along her last-known route. There's a chance the abduction was recorded. At the very least, you should be able to verify if she was where she was supposed to be."

"I can try. Send me the info."

"On it. There's one other thing. I'm forwarding you a video that was received from her kidnappers. There's a voice-over that's been altered to disguise the speaker's identity. Any chance you can peel away the effects so we can hear the person's real voice?"

"I'm not a sound guy, but I know a few good ones I can reach out to."

"No outsiders. This needs to be kept between you and me."

"I guess there are a few things I can try. But I can't promise anything."

"I have confidence in you."

"Gee. Thanks, Dad. I'll let you know when I have something."

The rest of the drive was made to the jazz coming from the Porsche's speakers and the feel of the wind blowing through Teddy's hair.

It took him two hours to reach his house in the Hollywood Hills. There, he retrieved several items from his safe, including a pair of handguns, a rifle, tracking and audio bugs, lock picks, zip ties, and a few electronic devices he thought might come in handy.

He hoped none of them would be necessary, but it was always better to be prepared.

12

REBECCA NOVAK ROLLED ONTO HER BACK AND groaned. Her head ached like she'd been drinking all night, though it had been years since she'd done something that stupid.

She reached for the bottle of water she always kept on her nightstand but found only air.

She opened her eyes and then slammed them shut again at the brightness.

Why had Carl turned on the lights?

With more care this time, she eased her eyelids apart.

Her nightstand wasn't there.

She bolted upright, then swayed at the sudden wave of vertigo. Once her head stopped spinning, she looked around.

There was a very good reason her nightstand

was missing. She wasn't in her bedroom. Rather, she was in a small, windowless room with bare concrete walls. The only items in the space were the cot she was on, a small table, and a portable toilet in the corner.

What the hell? Where am—

It all came rushing back.

The man next to her car.

Rebecca being forced into his vehicle.

A hand clamping down over her face.

And the slow foggy drift into unconsciousness.

After that, she remembered nothing until now.

Before she could think about what it all meant, something banged against the door. She shot a look toward it, sending a fresh spike of dizziness into her head.

The latch released and the door swung open. A man entered holding a gun. He wore a white plastic mask over his face that had holes cut out for his eyes and mouth.

Ignoring her weakened state, she pushed to her feet. "Who are you? What do you want?"

Without a word, the man shoved her back onto the bed with a simple flick of his hand and motioned for her not to move.

A second masked man walked in, carrying a bag of what smelled like fast food. After he set it on the table, both he and his armed companion left.

Rebecca hurried to the door, but it slammed

shut before she could get there. She raised a fist to bang against it, but then lowered it when she heard voices outside.

One of her kidnappers laughed. When the other made a comment that she couldn't understand, another memory hit her. In the kidnappers' car as she was losing consciousness, she'd heard two men speaking in something that had sounded like Croatian. The voice beyond the door was using the same language.

Were her kidnappers from Croatia?

She shuffled back to the cot and sat.

Why would someone from her husband's home country take her hostage?

She turned the question over in her head. But no matter what angle she looked at it from, the answer eluded her.

13

BY SIX A.M., TEDDY WAS UP AND READY TO GET BACK to work. His drive back from Hollywood had gone smoothly, landing him in Santa Barbara around three a.m. Getting only a few hours of sleep was nothing new for him. In his former life as an intelligence operative, there had been plenty of nights when he hadn't slept at all. Three hours of shut-eye felt like a luxury in comparison.

A check of his emails revealed that in addition to the normal flood of production-related messages, he had one from Kevin, asking Teddy to call as soon as he woke up.

"Finally," Kevin answered.

"Why, Kevin, I didn't know you cared so much. Have you been sitting by your phone, waiting for me to call?"

"No, of course not." Kevin paused. "Well, maybe a little."

"What do you have for me?"

"For starters, I figured out Rebecca Novak's route before she went missing."

"Please tell me you found video of the kidnapping."

"I wish I could, but no. I was able to piece together where she went, though. Security camera footage shows that she stopped at the hospital first, then a drugstore, and then the wine shop you mentioned. From there, she went to a picture framing place and then the flower shop."

"And after that?"

"I don't know. Her car left the flower shop, and a few blocks later traveled into a dead zone. I searched around to find where she came out of it, but there was no sign of her."

"Are you saying she's within that dead zone?"

"I'm saying I saw her car enter it but not leave. That doesn't mean it's still there now. I only checked a two-hour window from the point I lost track of her. The car could have left any time after that. Or maybe it was put on a flatbed, covered, and driven out before that."

Teddy frowned. He'd been hoping for more. "I'd like to see what you found. Can you send me the clips?"

"Hold on."

In the background, Teddy heard the distinct **swoosh** of an email being sent.

"The links should be in your inbox now. I figured you'd want them, so I prepped them ahead of time."

"Gold star for you."

"I've also included a link to that audio you wanted me to clean up. It's just a first pass, so don't get excited. I'll take another crack at it after I get some rest."

"Kevin, you're making me regret every bad thing I've ever said about you."

"What?"

"Nothing. Any other surprises?"

"You've said bad things about me?"

"Kevin, keep up. We've moved on. Anything else?"

"Um, well, kinda. I'm not sure how important it is, though."

"Let's hear it."

"The kidnapping video had metadata attached that confirmed it had been shot on the same day it was sent. It also indicated the video had been recorded by an older model iPhone. No serial number or phone number, though. That's it."

"Sounds like you had a busy night."

Kevin yawned as he said, "I've had worse."

"Get some sleep. We'll talk again later."

Teddy hung up and checked his email again. Kevin's new message had arrived.

Teddy clicked on a link labeled **Audio Clean-up Attempt #1**. The voice of the kidnapper was clearer than in the original recording, but not by much. Teddy listened to it several times but still couldn't tell if the speaker was a man or a woman.

He clicked next through the security footage links. At first, he thought the kidnapping had occurred after Rebecca left the flower shop and had driven into the area with no cameras. But as he rewatched the clip of her car leaving the parking lot, he wasn't so sure.

The shot was taken from a restaurant across the street. Kevin had included a note that he could find no cameras in the flower shop parking area.

Teddy paused the clip at the point where Rebecca's Mercedes was about to turn onto the street. Try as he might, he couldn't tell if it was her behind the wheel or someone else. He enlarged the image, but that didn't help. The glare off the windshield made it impossible to see more than a partial silhouette of the driver. Which meant he couldn't rule out any possibility just yet.

His phone vibrated, alerting him to a new text message. It was the contact info for Freeman's men who would be joining Teddy that morning.

Teddy sent both men a text, introducing himself as George Samuels, a fellow security consultant, and letting them know they'd be working with him today. He included the address of where and when he wanted to meet.

After transforming into Billy Barnett, he grabbed the garment bag in which he'd put some clothes for later and headed downstairs. Instead of taking his Porsche, he checked out one of the more anonymous production sedans from a production assistant who met him in the lobby, and drove to the set for his promised visit.

BY DAWN, KORDO WAS PARKED BACK ON THE STREET near the Santa Barbara Hills Hotel.

After he'd realized he'd been spotted the night before, he'd returned to the Italian restaurant, in time to be there when the other man from the meeting at the lawyer's office left. Kordo had followed him to the hotel. He waited to see if the man would come back out, but when he hadn't after a few hours, Kordo assumed he was staying there. After making a quick stop at the flower shop where he and Neno had grabbed Rebecca, to make sure no evidence of what they'd done had been left behind, he headed back to their hideout.

He believed there was at least a decent chance the man in the Porsche was staying at the hotel, too. Hence his return trip this morning. If it turned out that wasn't the case, he was certain that the Porsche driver's friend would lead Kordo to him.

Kordo's instincts proved correct again, because at a few minutes after seven a.m., the hotel door opened, and the Porsche driver exited.

The man handed the valet a slip of paper, but when the valet returned, he wasn't driving the sports car. Rather, he brought a far less flashy dark blue sedan. Kordo thought it must be for someone else until the Porsche driver climbed inside.

Interesting. How many cars had the man brought to the hotel?

Kordo followed him, taking even more care not to be spotted than he had the night before. The sedan drove to an area north of downtown and parked on a side street. Oddly, several other people were also climbing out of vehicles, as if they had also just arrived.

Kordo grabbed a spot near the end of the block and continued his pursuit on foot. He made it as far as the corner but could go no farther, due to the road being blocked off.

The Porsche driver did not have the same problem. He walked up to the security checkpoint and was waved straight through.

Kordo looked around, trying to figure out what was going on. Down the street, beyond the roadblock, he could see several large trucks. At least one had a crew removing equipment of some kind.

On Kordo's side of the barrier, a group of people were standing at the corner opposite of where he stood. Some were talking excitedly, while others peeked at the area beyond the roadblock.

Kordo walked over to a man near the back, standing by himself.

"Hey. Do you know what is going on here?"

The man glanced at him and huffed. "What does it look like? They're shooting a movie."

Kordo's eyebrows shot up in surprise, then he chuckled to himself. A film production **did** make a weird kind of sense. He was on this job because of the Novaks' involvement with filmmakers in Croatia, after all. The movie here would explain Carl Novak's connection to the Porsche driver.

Kordo spotted the driver, about a half block down, talking to a woman, and he pointed at him. "He looks important. Is he one of the actors?"

"Who?" The man looked down the street. "Him? An actor? You've got to be kidding. That's Billy Barnett. He's the producer."

Kordo silently repeated the name, thanked the man, and headed back to his car.

14

AFTER POURING HIMSELF A COFFEE, TEDDY LOOKED over the breakfast choices on the craft services table. He was deciding between a bagel and a piece of fruit when Stacy found him.

"You actually made it."

"I said I would, didn't I?"

"Yes, but it wouldn't have been the first time something came up that changed your plans."

"Are you calling me unreliable?"

"I'm calling you busy."

"Very diplomatic, Stacy. If I didn't know any better, I'd say you were angling for a raise."

"I would never say no to that." She pulled several sheets of paper out of a folder. "I have today's schedule, if you'd like a copy."

"Why don't you hold on to that. I won't be staying long."

"You won't? Do you still want an update?"

"I can't think of a better way to spend what little time I'll be here."

Stacy's eyes narrowed. "You don't sound like you're being sincere."

"Me? Why, I'm both hurt by what you're implying and impressed by your perceptiveness. Maybe you **do** deserve a raise." He took a sip from his cup. "How about we keep this simple. I've read all your daily reports. Is there anything that wasn't in yesterday's that I should know about?"

She shook her head, unable to hide her disappointment. "No. It was all there."

"That means you're doing a great job of keeping me informed."

"I hope so."

"There is one thing you can do for me."

She perked up. "What's that?"

"Point me to the trailers."

Stacy escorted him to the parking lot where the cast and makeup trailers were located. After she left, he walked around the set for several minutes, shaking hands and talking to cast and crew. Once he felt he'd done enough to fulfill Peter's request that he make an appearance, he went into Mark Weldon's trailer and locked the door.

Using the makeup kit, he transformed himself into a hardened Santa Barbara police detective he named Wesley Thompson. He completed the look by donning the slacks and sports jacket he'd brought in the garment bag. He checked himself in the mirror and was happy with the results, ducking out of the trailer when nobody was around.

Instead of returning to the production sedan the same way he'd come, he took the long way around the cordoned-off area, to avoid running into anyone he knew on set. Though there was next to no chance someone would realize he was in disguise, it was best not to tempt fate whenever possible.

He used the information he'd received from Kevin to drive Rebecca's exact route. As he did, he kept an eye out for her car, but he didn't see it anywhere. When he reached the flower shop, he pulled into the lot and parked.

There were spaces for twenty vehicles. Half were along the back of the building, and the other half along a cinder-block wall that enclosed the lot.

Teddy climbed out and scanned the area. Given that Kevin had found no indication of cameras covering the lot, he was surprised to spot two cameras mounted to the back of the shop. They were aimed so that together they covered the entire parking area.

Maybe they were only props. Some businesses did that to discourage would-be thieves, without incurring the cost of a full video surveillance system.

But when he went up close to check them, he saw that wasn't the case here. There were cables running from the back of the cameras, cables that had been cut.

As he walked into the shop, an older woman behind the counter smiled at him. "Good morning. How may I help you?"

Teddy flashed his fake police badge. "Detective Thompson. Santa Barbara PD."

Her smile slipped as her eyes widened. "What can I do for you, Detective?"

"I'm looking into some vandalism that occurred in your neighborhood. I notice you have cameras in your parking lot. I was hoping I could get a look at your security footage."

"Oh. That depends. When did this occur?"

"Yesterday afternoon."

"I'm so sorry. I don't think I can be of any help. The cameras stopped working at some point yesterday. I haven't had time to figure out what's wrong with them."

"Do you know exactly when your system went down?"

"I'm not sure. It was fine when I opened yesterday morning, but when I checked the monitor before I went home, there was only static."

"Do you save your footage?"

"Yes. On a hard drive."

"May I take a look? It's possible one of the suspects was captured before your cameras glitched."

"Sure. If you'd like."

She led him into a small room in the back, where the monitoring equipment was kept. As she stepped inside, she sucked in a breath. "It's gone."

Teddy entered behind her. "What's gone?"

"The hard drive. Someone took it."

She moved to the side so he could see. Below the monitor was an empty slot, with a couple of unattached cables hanging through it.

"You didn't move it?"

"No."

"What about one of your employees?"

"I only have two, and they would have had no reason to come in here. But I'll ask them when they get in."

"Have you noticed anything else missing?"

"No. Nothing."

"You said you checked the monitor before you left last night. Are you sure the drive wasn't gone then?"

"It couldn't have been. I would have noticed."

"Did anyone leave after you?"

Another shake of her head. "I closed up last night and opened this morning." She glanced at the empty spot. "Why would someone break in and only steal my hard drive?"

"That's an excellent question. Since I'm on another case, I'll call this in and have someone come out to investigate. Thank you for your time."

Back in his car, Teddy call the SBPD to report the theft, then scanned the lot again. Every instinct told him that this was where Rebecca had been kidnapped.

He called Kevin but was sent straight to voicemail. The hacker was probably still sleeping.

At the beep, Teddy said, "I need you to try enhancing the image of Rebecca Novak's Mercedes when it left the flower shop parking lot. I don't think she was the one driving."

15

TEDDY ARRIVED AT THE SHOPPING PLAZA AHEAD OF
schedule. As anticipated, the lot was busy but
not full.

He parked in the less crowded corner he'd
preselected and used the extra time to alter the
look of Detective Wesley Thompson into that
of an overweight, middle-aged man. As a final
touch, he added a bushy mustache and a pair of
black-framed glasses.

Two minutes prior to the rendezvous time, a
van pulled into the slot next to Teddy. Painted on
the side was the logo for Strategic Services.

The driver of the van rolled down his window
as Teddy climbed out of his car.

"Mr. Samuels?"

"That's me."

"I'm Daniel Rivera." Rivera pointed across the cab to the man in the passenger seat. "And he's Kyle Hansen. Shall we get going?"

Hansen climbed into the back of the van, and Teddy took his vacated seat up front.

"Did Mr. Freeman brief you on what's going on?"

"In broad strokes," Rivera said.

Teddy filled in the details of his plan while they drove to the Novaks' estate.

When they pulled up to the gate across the driveway, a voice came over the intercom. "May I help you?"

Teddy leaned across the cab. "We're here to do a home security audit. I believe you're expecting us."

"Drive up to the house and park on the right side, please."

The gate swung open, and they followed the driveway in.

A man in a smart-looking suit exited the house and approached them as they climbed out of the van.

"Good morning, gentlemen. I'm Andrew Vulin, the manager of the Novaks' estate. Mr. Novak told me to give you whatever help you need."

Teddy shook his hand. "George Samuels. We're only doing an assessment today. Which means we need to check out your current security system, including window and door contacts, any cameras, things like that."

"Where would you like to start?"

"How about inside?"

"Follow me."

When they walked into the large foyer, Vulin introduced them to the five other members of the staff, all of whom were waiting there. "They can find me if you have questions."

Teddy, Rivera, and Hansen began their "assessment" of the house on the first floor.

They looked for signs of break-ins, or any clue as to how someone might have gained entrance in order to leave the notes. But after thoroughly scouring the interior on both floors and checking the doors and windows from the outside, they found absolutely nothing.

While Rivera and Hansen packed up the ladders they'd used, Teddy found Vulin in a small office off the kitchen. "I think we have everything we need. I hope we didn't disturb your staff too much."

"I haven't heard any complaints."

"Please let Mr. Novak know that we'll be in touch."

"Of course. Do you need someone to show you out?"

"I'm good. Thanks."

Once the van was on the road again, Teddy said, "Thoughts?"

Rivera answered without hesitation. "I don't believe anyone broke into that house."

"Neither do I," Hansen agreed.

Teddy nodded. "Then that makes three of us."

"Only means one thing then . . ." Rivera said.

"It was an inside job," Teddy finished.

16

"ACTION," PETER SAID.

Adriene rushed out of the building, on the verge of tears.

Tessa hurried right behind her and grabbed Adriene's arm. "Wait."

"Let me go." Adriene tried to pull free, but Tessa held tight.

"Please, come back inside. Just give him a chance."

"Give him a chance?" Adriene looked at Tessa as if Tessa had lost her mind. "We've spent our whole lives giving him chances. I'm done."

"He's trying. You don't understand what he's—"

"I don't care." Adriene yanked her arm from Tessa. "You shouldn't care, either. Do you even remember what he did to you? All the promises he never kept? What he did to Mom and Dad?"

Tessa looked as if she had no idea how to answer.

"I never want to see him again. And you shouldn't, either." Adriene stared at Tessa for a beat, then turned and hurried away.

This time, Tessa did not follow.

"And cut." Peter moved out from behind a monitor, a broad smile on his face. "Adriene, that was terrific. Exactly what I wanted."

Adriene tried her best not to blush but failed. She and Tessa were playing the nieces of Mark's character, whose lives have been upended by Tyler Storm's attempt at making amends.

Peter turned to his crew. "Camera? Sound?" When he received confirmation that both were good, he said, "Let's set up for the close-ups."

Tessa walked over to Adriene and put an arm around her. "That felt great, didn't it?"

"It did."

"We make a good team."

The second assistant director approached them. "We'll be back up in about fifteen minutes. Let's get you two into makeup for touch-ups."

MATTHEW STOOD AT THE BACK OF A GROUP OF FANS, watching as Tessa and Adriene were escorted away from the set. He was too far away to have heard the dialogue, but he had seen Tessa's face. Her ability to say so much with only a look continued to amaze him.

He couldn't be prouder of her.

The thought of telling her in person how he felt sent a rush of pleasure down his spine.

Soon, he promised himself.

From his pocket, he pulled out the shooting schedule he'd stolen that morning. The production was running a little late, but not by much. They had only a few more shots to get before they'd call it a day.

Which meant it was almost time to set his plan in motion.

"Hey, what's that?"

Matthew looked up, annoyed. A man had moved in next to him and was looking at the schedule.

He was the second person today who'd tried to engage Matthew in conversation. The first was a fool who thought Billy Barnett was one of the actors. Billy Barnett, a movie actor? How ridiculous was that?

This new guy wore a black T-shirt with a button pinned to it that read: I LOVE YOU TESSA. In the background, behind the type, was a photo of the nosy good-for-nothing posing with Tessa. One of those selfies fans liked to take.

Matthew instantly disliked him.

"Is that from the production?" The superfan pointed at the schedule. "Can I see it?"

Matthew wanted to stuff the paper in his pocket and walk away, but he was keenly aware of the man's eyes on him. Remaining unnoticed was a crucial part of Matthew's plan, but this creep was paying him too much attention. That was a problem that needed to be rectified immediately.

"Sure." He held out the schedule. "Take a look."

The man grinned. "Thanks."

Matthew glanced around to make sure no one else was paying attention to them, then whispered, "I also have a script."

"What?" From the way the guy gawked at him, one would think Matthew had told him he'd found the holy grail. It was just the reaction Matthew had hoped for.

"It's in my car. I can show it to you if you're interested."

"Hell yeah, I'm interested."

"Cool. My car's not far." As they turned the corner, Matthew held out a hand. "I'm Matthew."

"Justin."

"Good to meet you, Justin. Nice button."

"Thanks. I made it myself."

Matthew led him to the block where he'd parked.

"This is it," he said, when they reached his car. "The script's in the trunk."

He walked Justin to the back of the sedan. After sticking his key into the lock, he pretended to turn it, then grimaced in annoyance when the hatch didn't pop open.

"Sorry, the lock gets sticky sometimes."

He fiddled with it again, then pulled the key out.

"Wait here. I've got a spare that works better."

"Sure." Justin was so excited at the prospect of seeing a script for **Storm's Eye** that he didn't suspect a thing.

Matthew climbed into his front passenger seat and popped open the glove compartment. Under the car manual was a small black case that contained three syringes and two glass containers full of clear liquid. He filled one syringe, put the case back, then quickly removed his car key from his key ring so that it wouldn't appear to be the same one.

When he returned to Justin, he held up the key. "Got it."

This time he turned it all the way, and the trunk opened.

The space inside was empty.

"I don't see it," Justin said.

"It's under the carpet, on top of the spare. I was worried someone might break in and steal it."

"Oh. Good thinking. Some people will do just about anything these days."

"Too true. Can you pull the corner up?"

Matthew pointed at where he meant. "That's the easiest way to get underneath."

Justin reached into the trunk, his smile wide in anticipation. As soon as Matthew had a clear shot, he shoved the needle into the man's neck and pushed the plunger.

Justin spun around. "What the—" Before he could get another word out, he staggered against the bumper. "Whaa . . ."

"Don't fight it."

Justin's eyelids fluttered as he tried but failed to focus on Matthew.

Matthew grabbed him and eased him down so that he sat on the rim of the trunk. "There you go."

Justin blinked again, his eyes shutting longer each time.

"Everything's going to be all right." It wasn't a lie, at least not in regards to Matthew.

Justin's lids drooped until they closed again, this time for good.

Matthew eased him onto his side and rolled him into the trunk. Nice and neat.

After he shut the top, he looked around to make sure they were still alone. He needn't have worried. He'd parked on a deserted side street, next to a tall chain-link fence overgrown with ivy. On the other side of the road was the windowless wall of a plumbing supply business. No one had seen him.

He returned casually to the street corner where the fans were gathered and watched the crew film the last two shots of the day. He then made his way to the street where the production cars were parked.

It was time.

17

BACK ON THE SET, STACY KNOCKED ON ADRIENE'S trailer door. "Ready whenever you are."

"Coming," Adriene called from inside.

Stacy crossed to Tessa's trailer and repeated the process.

A few moments later, the two actresses stepped outside, wearing the street clothes they'd come to the set in that morning.

Tessa put one arm around Adriene's back and the other around Stacy's. "I was thinking seafood tonight. How does that sound?"

Adriene's eyes lit up. "I am definitely in."

Tessa looked at Stacy. "Okay with you?"

"More than okay." Stacy wasn't sure she would ever get used to the fact that she was not only working with the famous Tessa Tweed and rising star Adriene Adele, but was also becoming fast friends with them.

"Let's give ourselves forty-five minutes to freshen up once we get back to the hotel, then meet in the lobby."

They headed down the block where they'd been shooting that day to a hidden pathway that wound between buildings to the road where Stacy's production van was parked.

They had barely started down the path when Tessa stopped short and searched through her purse.

"Forget something?" Adriene asked.

Tessa sighed and closed her bag. "I left my phone in my trailer."

"I can run back and get it for you," Stacy offered.

"It's my mistake. I'll do it."

"I don't mind."

"Someday, someone is going to take advantage of that good-natured helpfulness of yours, but it's not going to be me."

"How about I at least bring the van around, and you can meet us at the end of the block. It'll save you some time."

"Wonderful. Billy better be careful because I might steal you from him."

MATTHEW WATCHED FROM DOWN THE BLOCK AS Tessa crossed the street in the company of Adriene

Adele and the same woman who'd gone to dinner with them the night before.

This was it. The moment he'd been waiting for was upon him. He slipped his hand into the pocket of his hoodie and wrapped his fingers around the remote.

When he was sure that Tessa and her friends had reached the path they used to get to their vehicle, he jogged to the end of the street where the walkway let out. He then slowed his pace and headed down the sidewalk, his body tingling in anticipation. If he had his timing correct, he should arrive at the spot where the pathway hit the street at the same time Tessa did.

He was so sure that he'd timed everything perfectly that he almost froze in mid-step when he got there, with no sign of Tessa or her friends.

Out of the corner of his eye, he checked down the path. It was clear all the way to where it curved out of sight.

Had he been wrong? Had they **not** been heading this way?

Before his panic spiraled out of control, the sound of footsteps drifted toward him. Then he heard a woman's voice that he was positive belonged to Adriene Adele.

He took a deep, relieved breath. They'd been walking slower than he'd anticipated, that was all.

Everything was fine.

He couldn't stay there and wait for them,

though, that would be too obvious. It would mean a change to his plan, but only a small one.

He began walking again.

When he'd gone two car lengths, he heard the women laugh as they reached the street behind him.

He smiled and pressed the button on the remote.

18

THE PATH WAS WIDE ENOUGH FOR STACY AND Adriene to walk side by side.

"If the rest of filming goes as smoothly as today, do you think we might finish on location ahead of schedule?" Adriene asked.

"If we do, I think it would be the first time in the history of filmmaking that will have happened."

They laughed as they stepped off the path and onto the sidewalk.

"Wishful thinking, I—"

Gunshots echoed down the street, cutting Adriene off.

Before either woman could do anything more than jump in surprise, a male voice shouted, "Get down!"

As they dropped to a crouch next to a parked

car, a young man rushed over to them. "Lie on the ground! Less chance of"—he looked around, confused, before finishing what he'd been saying—"getting hit."

Stacy and Adriene lowered to the concrete, next to the car. The man draped himself over them a second before another volley of gunfire erupted.

Adriene trembled in fear. Stacy wasn't doing much better, but she grabbed her friend's hand. "I'm right here. We'll get through this."

They waited for a third round of gunshots, frozen in place. When it didn't materialize, the man cautiously lifted himself off them.

"Stay here. I'll check if it's clear."

Stacy looked up in alarm. "It's not safe."

"Don't worry. I'll be careful."

MATTHEW MADE A SHOW OF SCANNING THE STREET before he jogged over to the narrow park that ran down the other side. He was projecting a façade of concern, but inside he was raging.

Where was Tessa?

She should have been with the other two when they reached the street.

He was supposed to save **her,** not her friends.

He contemplated leaving then and there, but if he did that he'd risk people thinking he'd been involved with the gunfire. He wouldn't be able to show his face around the film shoot again and that would ruin everything. He'd just have to follow through with the plan for now and come up with another way to get close to Tessa later.

He "searched" the park, pretending to make sure no danger remained. As he did, he collected the homemade device that had created the sounds of the gunshots, slipping it into his pocket.

Once he'd put on enough of a show, he returned to Adriene and the other woman. "It's okay. They're gone."

The women slowly lifted their heads and peeked at the street.

The one whose name he didn't know looked skeptical. "Are you sure?"

"There's no one here but us."

Both women finally relaxed.

He crouched beside them. "Are you two all right?"

"If you don't count the fact that my heart is about to burst out of my chest, I'm fine."

Adriene nodded. "What she said."

From the pathway behind them came the thuds of running footsteps. Two armed security officers from the set rushed onto the sidewalk a moment later and looked around.

When they spotted the two women and Matthew, they hurried over. One of them pointed his weapon at Matthew.

"Sir, back away from them. Now."

Matthew raised his hands and did as ordered.

"It wasn't him," Adriene said. "He's the one who saved us."

The guard hesitated before lowering his gun. "Are either of you hurt?"

"We're okay," the other woman said.

Matthew gestured to the street. "Whoever fired the gun was down that way. But they're gone now."

The guard glanced at his partner, who was scanning the street. "See anyone?"

"Looks clear. I think he's right."

The first guard helped the women to their feet. "Let's get you someplace safe."

He and his partner guided them toward the pathway. But before they'd gone more than a few steps, Adriene's friend looked back at Matthew. "You should come with us. It may not be safe to stay here."

"Oh, um, is that okay?"

"Of course it is."

"Then, sure. Thank you."

The woman held out her hand. "I'm Stacy. She's Adriene."

"Matthew. Matthew Wagner."

"Thanks for saving our lives, Matthew Wagner."

He stifled a grin. Maybe the situation wasn't as big of a disaster as he'd thought.

19

TEDDY PARKED HIS PORSCHE IN FRONT OF THE
roadblock at the end of the street where the film
shoot had been that day.

As he jumped out, a guard jogged over. "Hey,
you can't—" His eyes widened. "Oh, Mr. Barnett.
My apologies."

Teddy tossed him the keys. "Let me know if
you move it."

He ran through the gate and headed straight
to the trailer area, where more than a dozen
members of the cast and crew and several police
officers were gathered.

He'd been at the hotel, changing himself back
into Billy Barnett when he'd received a call about
the shooting.

He spotted Peter and made a beeline for him. "Is everyone okay?"

"Billy, I'm glad you're here. No one was hurt. The police doubt it had anything to do with the movie. I had someone take Tessa and Adriene back to the hotel. Stacy's still here, though."

"Where?"

"In my trailer."

With a nod of thanks, Teddy jogged to Peter's trailer and let himself in.

The moment she saw him, Stacy hopped to her feet. "Mr. Barnett. You didn't need to come."

"It's not every day someone shoots at my assistant."

"I don't think they were shooting **at** me."

"Close enough. Are you okay?"

"A little rattled, but I'll be fine."

Teddy looked at the man beside Stacy, who had followed her lead and risen to his feet. "Who is this?"

The guy looked to be in his late twenties or early thirties, and seemed vaguely familiar, though Teddy felt sure he'd never met him.

"This is Matthew Wagner. He's the one who saved Adriene and me."

Matthew looked a little embarrassed. "I don't think you could call it saving you. All I did was tell you to get down."

"**And** acted as our shield."

"Well . . ."

Teddy stuck out his hand. "Sounds like you went above and beyond to me. Thank you." They shook. "We're all very grateful."

Over the next few minutes, Stacy told Teddy her version of events.

"Have the police talked to you yet?"

"Yes. Both of us."

"Then why are you still here?"

"They asked us to wait in case they had any other questions."

"Give me a minute."

Outside, he asked the first officer he found to point him to the person in charge of the investigation. The cop nodded toward a man in a brown suit, talking to one of the movie's security guards.

Teddy walked over. "Sorry for butting in, but I'm Billy Barnett, the film's producer."

Though the detective tried to hide it, Billy saw a familiar starstruck glimmer in the man's eye. "I'm Detective Steve Alverez."

"I don't want to bother you, Detective, but do you have a moment?"

Alverez glanced at the security guard. "If I have any other questions, I'll let you know." He turned back to Billy as the guard walked off. "How can I help you?"

"I was wondering if you've been able to identify the shooter yet."

"It's still an open investigation."

"I take that as a no, then."

Alverez gave him a closed-lipped smile but said nothing.

Teddy pulled out his business card and handed it to the detective. "When you do find out, I'd appreciate a call."

"Of course." Alverez slipped the card carefully into his pocket.

"Thanks, Detective. One more question. Would it be okay if my assistant and the man waiting with her went home? It's been a long day for them."

Alverez consulted his notepad. "Stacy Lange and Matthew Wagner?"

"Yes."

"I have their contact info, so sure, they can go."

"Appreciate it."

A POLICE OFFICER ESCORTED STACY AND MATTHEW to Stacy's VAN, then went back to the set. Other officers were scattered along the street, examining the crime scene.

"I can't thank you enough for what you did," Stacy told Matthew.

"I'm just happy everyone's all right."

"Listen, I don't know if you'd be interested, but we're in town for another two weeks. If you're around, come by, and I'll get you on the set."

"Really?" Matthew said, genuinely surprised. If he could get onto the set, maybe all wasn't lost, after all.

"It's the least I can do."

"That would be fantastic. Thank you. I'm actually free tomorrow if that would work."

"Great. Give me your number. In the morning, I'll text you where to meet us."

20

TEDDY HUNG AROUND THE SET FOR ANOTHER HOUR, hoping one of the cops would divulge what they'd learned so far. But the only additional information he gleaned came from a rookie cop who was working crowd control.

"You saw the video, didn't you?" the officer asked.

"What video?"

"Of the shooting."

"There's video?"

The cop bobbed his head side to side. "Sort of. Here." He opened a video-sharing app on his phone to show Teddy. "A fan was standing down the street, trying to get shots of the stars as they left. This was uploaded before we even arrived at the scene."

The title of the video was **Adriene Adele**

Escapes Death! It already had more than five thousand views.

The shot of the street was focused on the back of a man walking away from the camera. Matthew, if Teddy wasn't mistaken.

A voice off-screen said, "I don't think he's anybody."

"Are you sure?" a second voice asked.

"I don't recognize him. Do you?"

"Nah. I guess you're right."

Matthew grew smaller in frame as the shot started zooming out. It had widened enough to catch Adriene and Stacy exiting the pathway onto the sidewalk.

"Ooh! That's Adriene A—"

Gunshots drowned out the rest of what the unseen voice said.

The image jerked around as whoever was holding the camera took cover. The person maintained enough awareness, though, to keep the lens aimed at Adriene, Stacy, and Matthew.

The rest of the action played out exactly as Stacy had described it.

When it became clear Teddy would learn nothing else, he returned to his car. He'd just settled into the driver's seat when he received a text from Kevin.

This is as far as I can push it without the audio degrading beyond recognition.

Teddy tapped the provided link, and the kidnapping video played on his screen. Though there was still some distortion to the voice, the audio was cleaned up enough for him to tell that the speaker was male and had a European accent.

As he started to listen to it again, his phone rang with a call from Kevin.

The instant Teddy accepted it, Kevin said, "You're going to want to see this right away."

"See what?"

Teddy was answered by the vibration of another text message, also from Kevin. He put the call on speaker and opened the message. It contained a link that took him to a still image from the footage of Rebecca's Mercedes leaving the flower shop parking lot. Unlike before, where a glare on the windshield prevented the driver from being seen, this time the person behind the wheel was visible.

"That's definitely not Rebecca," Teddy said.

The picture was grainy from the manipulation Kevin had done, so details were lacking. Even so, there was enough to see that the driver was a man and to get a decent idea of what he looked like. Teddy was certain he had never seen him before.

One thing for sure, though, the flower shop was where the kidnapping had gone down.

"This is great, Kevin. Thank you. And for the audio, too. I told you you could do it."

"I'm adding the skill to my résumé as we speak."

"That's the spirit. Listen, do you think you can get into the Santa Barbara Police Department server?" It was a task Teddy could have done himself, but he was short on time.

Kevin snorted. "I'm going to pretend that's not a serious question. What do you need?"

21

"MR. BILLY BARNETT," VULIN ANNOUNCED, THEN moved to the side so Teddy could enter the Novaks' library.

Novak threw Teddy a quick glance from where he stood by one of the windows. He looked exhausted. Teddy doubted he'd slept since his wife disappeared the previous afternoon.

Mori didn't appear much better. He sat on one of the couches, dark circles under his eyes, and his hair mussed, like he'd been running his hand through it nonstop. On the coffee table sat a laptop.

The lawyer waved Teddy over. "We received another video."

"When?"

"A few minutes ago."

Teddy checked his watch. It was a quarter after six. That was approximately the same time yesterday's video had arrived.

"Play it for me."

The shot was almost identical to the one in the previous video. The cot, the concrete wall behind it, and even the audio were unchanged.

There were two obvious differences, however. Instead of the number five written on the piece of paper taped to the wall, today the number was four.

The second change was Rebecca herself. Now, she sat on the cot, staring at the camera.

She looked both scared and exhausted. What she did not look was defeated. Nor did she appear to have any obvious injuries.

Novak joined them and pointed at the number on the wall. "It has to be a countdown, right?"

Teddy nodded. "That would be my guess."

"Then we only have four days. That's not much time. Has your friend made any progress yet?"

Teddy answered by pulling out his phone and playing the unfiltered audio from the previous video for them. When it was done, he said, "Do either of you recognize the voice?"

Mori shook his head right away, while Novak took a couple of seconds before saying, "No."

When Teddy showed them the enhanced

picture of the Mercedes leaving the flower shop, Novak gasped. "That's Rebecca's car." His gaze whipped to Teddy. "Is he the one who kidnapped her?"

"Either that or he's working with those who did. Do you know him?"

Novak took the phone from Teddy and studied the picture.

His breath caught as if he did indeed know the man. But just as fast, the spark of recognition faded. With a frown, he shook his head. "I've never seen him."

He handed the phone back to Teddy.

"Are you positive? For a moment there, you looked like you did."

"He looks a little like someone I used to know, that's all. When I was young."

"Who?"

"My friend Leon."

"He'd be older now. Are you sure it's not him?"

"I'm positive. Leon Janic died when we were teenagers."

"BILLY! JOIN ME?"

Teddy, who had just returned to the Santa Barbara Hills Hotel after visiting the Novak house, was walking through the lobby when he heard the sound of Peter's voice. Looking around, he spotted Peter sitting in the hotel bar, a martini in his hand.

Teddy walked over and took a seat at Peter's table. "Drinking alone? That's not like you."

Peter signaled the waiter and pointed at his glass. "He'll take one of these, too." He turned back to Teddy. "It's only drinking if you actually drink. This is my first and I haven't even touched it yet. Besides, you're here now, so I'm not drinking alone."

Teddy had seldom ever seen Peter anywhere close to being rattled. He was verging on that now. But that was to be expected. Not every shoot day ended in an actual shooting.

Peter picked up his glass, then set it down again without taking a drink. "Have you heard anything from the police? Do they have a suspect?"

"Nothing new since I left the set."

"You don't think the shooter was after one of our people, do you?"

Teddy didn't have enough information to know the answer to that yet, but he knew that wasn't what Peter needed to hear. "I doubt it. But we'll know more after the police finish their investigation."

"Should we beef up security?"

"I was planning on calling Mike Freeman when I got to my room to do just that."

"Okay. Good." Peter visibly relaxed. "So

I don't need to push the shoot back a day or two, then?"

"Only if you want to."

Peter shook his head. "The show must go on. Plus, I think it would be better for everyone to keep working."

"I couldn't agree more."

The waiter returned with Teddy's martini and then left.

For the first time since Teddy sat down, Peter cracked a smile. "You know, since we'll still be shooting tomorrow, I'll need Mark on set first thing in the morning."

"Mark is a pro. I'm sure he'll be there."

Teddy lifted his glass and took a sip. As he set the drink down, his phone vibrated with a text from Kevin.

Check your email.

Teddy did. Kevin's email contained copies of everything the police had on their investigation of the shooting.

"Problem?" Peter asked.

Teddy looked up from his phone and shook his head. "Just some things I need to look over. I should head up to my room."

Peter pushed his still mostly full glass toward the middle of the table. "That's not a bad idea. I'll go up, too."

They rode the elevator up together, then headed to their respective suites.

IN HIS ROOM, TEDDY WENT THROUGH THE POLICE documents. It wasn't much. Without very much evidence, one of their theories was that the guns had been fired on a neighboring street, but Teddy was skeptical.

In the video taken by the fan, the shots were loud and unmuffled. If they'd come from another street, the sound would have been dampened by the buildings in the area.

While he hoped it was only a matter of Stacy and Adriene being in the wrong place at the wrong time, and despite what he'd said to Peter to reassure him, he couldn't ignore the possibility that the shooting had something to do with the movie.

He called Mike Freeman and brought him up to speed with the day's events.

"There's never a dull moment around you, is there?"

"What can I say? I have a magnetic personality."

"One that attracts killers and kidnappers, apparently."

"I'm concerned about security on set. It would be great if we could get some of your men here to augment the local crew."

"Consider it done."

"You know, I'd feel much better if your people were in charge overall, too."

"So would I. I'll send the two men who were with you yesterday. They're my best on the West Coast."

22

MATTHEW SHOULD HAVE BEEN TOO TIRED TO WAKE up early.

Disposing of Justin's body in the mountains north of Santa Barbara had taken much longer than he'd planned. He hadn't arrived back at the Airbnb he was renting until after two a.m.

And yet here he was, less than five hours later, standing in front of the closet, excited to pick out what he would wear for the day.

He fingered the sleeve of the dark blue Armani suit, hanging on the rack. It was the most expensive item of clothing he had ever owned. The only time he'd worn it had been at the tailors, when it was being altered. It was the outfit he planned to wear when he proclaimed his love to Tessa.

He'd be delusional if he thought that would

happen today, though. He wasn't even sure if he'd see her at all. And even if he did, he'd need time to build the bond between them before she realized that they were meant for each other. That she might not never entered his mind. To Matthew, their coming union was a foregone conclusion.

He settled for a button-down shirt and pair of slacks that were less flashy but still nice.

His phone buzzed as he put on his shoes. It was a text from Stacy, with the address where **Storm's Eye** would be shooting that day.

Wearing a smile he could barely contain, he grabbed his keys and headed for the door.

23

REBECCA'S EYES SNAPPED OPEN AT THE SOUND OF A sliding dead bolt.

Her stomach rumbled. She hadn't eaten since the greasy hamburger they'd left for her before she'd fallen asleep, so it had to be mealtime again. Breakfast, probably, though she had no idea what time it was since her room had no windows and the lights were kept on at all times.

The door swung open, and two of her captors entered, while the third remained in the hallway. All three wore the same white masks as before, but none carried the bag of food she expected.

"Get up," ordered the man who'd come in first.

She sighed and started to comply, but her efforts weren't fast enough for her captors. One of them snagged her arm and yanked her into a sitting position.

After he took a step back, she rubbed the spot where he'd clamped down on her and glared at him. "I was getting up. You didn't need to do that."

She could have been talking to a statue for all the good it did.

The other man taped something to the wall behind her.

She started to twist around to get a look, but the first man grabbed the sides of her head.

"No! Eyes toward door." The kidnapper in front of her turned her so that she faced the exit again and slapped her cheek hard. "Next time I will not be so nice."

She rubbed her face and scowled at him. "Fine. I get it. I won't look back. Happy?"

He responded with a grunt, but nothing more.

He and the other kidnapper stepped over to the doorway, without turning their backs to her. The man who'd slapped her raised a phone and aimed its lens at her.

Based on how he was holding it and for how long, Rebecca guessed he was shooting a video. She was tempted to say something but knew that would earn her more than a slap across the face.

When he lowered the phone again, the other guy pulled down whatever it was he'd put on the wall, then they exited the room.

The second man reappeared moments later, carrying a small carton of orange juice and a badly wrapped fast-food breakfast sandwich. He set it on the table and left, the door slamming shut behind him.

Rebecca stared at the sandwich but didn't pick it up, no longer hungry. It wasn't the slap that had taken away her appetite. It was the sudden feeling that her captors had no intention of ever letting her out of here.

She closed her eyes and grimaced. "Stop it," she hissed. "You can't let that happen. You can't let this room be the last place you ever see."

She told herself an opportunity to get away would come. It had to. And when it did, she needed to be ready.

Which meant she needed to stay strong.

She picked up the sandwich.

24

KORDO HAD ORIGINALLY PLANNED ON ARRIVING AT the film set first thing in the morning to stake out Billy Barnett. Getting the producer alone, finding out what he was up to, and eliminating him was his priority for the day, after all.

Neno, however, had something else in mind. "I want to shoot today's video before you leave. I don't want to be in a rush to get it done later."

By the time they had finished filming Rebecca and Kordo finally reached the set, production had already been underway for a few hours. At least he wouldn't be stuck sitting in his car, trying to catch a glimpse of the producer from a distance, like before. Today, he would be watching the filming from a much closer position.

Before heading back to their hideout last

evening, Kordo had paid a visit to the security company that was working on the production. There he'd swiped the uniform he was now wearing. He'd even found the ID of a man who looked vaguely like him. It wouldn't hold up to close scrutiny, but from a few yards away, no one would ever know the badge wasn't his.

He bypassed the check-in gate and sneaked onto the set.

One of the things he'd done in preparation was look up the main participants in the film online. This made it easy for him to recognize Tessa Tweed, Adriene Adele, Logan Chase, and the director Peter Barrington.

Barnett didn't seem to be around, though. If he'd been here and gone already, Kordo would give Neno hell for holding him up this morning. But the day was still young.

For now, he would continue acting like he was simply another guard on duty.

LOGAN CHASE LEANED BACK IN HIS CHAIR, SMIRKING. "I played his best friend, see. My death was what motivated him to seek revenge. So, I had to really sell it. Know what I mean? Which, of course, I did. You don't need to believe me, though. Just check the reviews. You could say, without my performance, the movie wouldn't have done half as well as it did."

Matthew faked looking interested. "Huh. I never thought of it that way."

They were in the cast seating area, a few yards behind the camera setup. Logan had been regaling Matthew with stories from his acting past. Matthew pretended to enjoy the conversation, while he sneaked looks around for Tessa. What he really thought of Logan Chase was that the guy was a complete bore. To keep a smile on his face, Matthew entertained thoughts of how he might make the actor disappear—permanently.

"I'm not saying the movie wouldn't have been as good without me, but I'm also not **not** saying that." Logan winked and laughed. "Kidding. I'm sure someone else could have done as good a job. Almost."

A security guard appeared from around the corner of one of the trailers behind Logan. There were more guards around today than yesterday, no doubt because of the mysterious gunshots. Matthew was about to look away and refocus on Logan when he realized there was something familiar about this one.

He didn't think the guard had been around during all the commotion last evening. But he was sure he had seen him somewhere.

It wasn't until the guard moved out of sight

that it hit him. He looked like the same guy who'd come up to Matthew yesterday morning and asked what was going on. The guy who had thought Billy Barnett was an actor.

When Matthew saw the guard again twenty minutes later, he revised his assessment. The man not only resembled the same guy from yesterday morning. He **was** the guy.

How he'd gone from not knowing anything about the movie to being an on-set security guard in less than twenty-four hours, Matthew had no idea.

"Hello there."

Matthew was so distracted by the guard that he hadn't even realized that someone had sat down on the other side of Logan and joined their conversation. When Matthew turned to look, his jaw almost dropped into his lap.

There, no more than four feet away, was Tessa.

He could barely breathe. She was even more beautiful in person than in any of the pictures he'd collected of her. Her eyes were friendly and inviting. Her smile radiated a warmth he wanted to wrap around himself forever.

Before he could say anything, Mark Weldon and Adriene Adele joined them.

"I do hope Logan hasn't been talking your ear off with one of his stories," Adriene said.

"I'm sorry?" It took Matthew a moment to realize she had been talking to him.

Tessa laughed. "Oh, my. He's been droning on so much you've zoned out, haven't you?"

Logan crossed his arms and raised an eyebrow.

"What are you upset about? It's not like what I said will get you to **stop** talking," Tessa teased.

His expression softened and he bobbed his head back and forth. "True."

"Tessa," Adriene said. "Have you met Matthew?"

"I haven't had the pleasure yet. Tessa Tweed."

Though Matthew had dreamed of this moment for a long time, he could hardly believe it was finally happening. He had to force himself to reach out to her extended hand. When they touched, a jolt of electricity rushed up his arm and into his chest. He was sure she had felt it, too.

"Hello. I'm Matthew Wagner." It was a miracle he was able to get the words out.

"You're the hero."

"I—I don't know if I'd call myself that."

He could feel her loosen her grip. He didn't want to let go, but he couldn't afford to let things get awkward, so he pulled his hand back. There would be plenty of time to hold her hand in the future.

"And this is Mark Weldon," Adriene said.

Mark was sitting a couple of seats down from Tessa, so Matthew had to get out of his seat to shake hands with him.

"Pleasure to meet you, Matthew. Thank you for what you did for Adriene and Stacy."

"Anyone would have done the same."

"Not true, but I appreciate your modesty."

Matthew smiled, then took his seat again. As he was trying to come up with something to say to Tessa, Ben Bacchetti appeared and hopped onto the empty seat beside her.

The warmth that had been coursing through Matthew's body turned frigid.

What the hell was Tessa's husband doing here?

He was supposed to be in Los Angeles.

Logan was apparently wondering the same thing. "I thought you went back to the studio."

"I did, but after I heard about what happened last night, I came right back."

Tessa scoffed in mock annoyance. "I told him that he was worrying over nothing. But he said he could work as easily from here as from his office." She kissed him on the cheek. "I'm certainly not going to complain about having him visit for a while."

"Matthew, are you all right?" Adriene asked.

"What?"

"You look like you're going to be sick."

Realizing he'd failed to keep his shock and revulsion from showing on his face, he plastered on a contrite smile. "Sorry, I think it was something I ate. But I'm okay now."

Saving him from further explanation, one of the assistant directors approached the group and said, "Mr. Weldon, Mr. Chase, we're ready for you."

Matthew stewed quietly as filming of the next scene got underway. While he was confident he would win Tessa's heart, he'd known from the start that doing so would not be easy, even without the presence of the man he hated more than anyone else. With Ben here, it would be much more of a challenge.

Or maybe not, he thought, as an idea hit him and melted away his anger.

Ben showing up here could actually be a good thing. Tessa's husband would be a problem no matter where he was, after all. The only way for Matthew to rid himself of the obstacle once and for all would be to remove Ben from the picture permanently. Something that would be much easier to arrange here in Santa Barbara than in Los Angeles.

Of course, it would have to be done in a way that could never be tied to Matthew, but how hard could that be? He'd taken care of that Justin guy without putting much thought into it, and that had gone off as smooth as silk.

Matthew grinned to himself. Ben's being here was not a problem at all. It was an opportunity.

He glanced at Tessa and her husband. They were watching the scene being filmed, Ben's hand resting on top of hers.

Enjoy it while you can. She won't be yours for much longer.

Movement at the craft services table beyond them caught Matthew's attention. The familiar guard was back.

Having observed him several times now, Matthew was convinced the guy wasn't a real guard but had somehow bluffed his way onto the set.

He wondered if he should turn him in. Doing so might earn Matthew even more praise from Tessa and her friends. But he decided against it.

If the real security guards weren't smart enough to notice that they had an imposter in their midst, why should Matthew do their job for them?

25

PETER TOOK A STEP AWAY FROM HIS MONITOR.
"That was great. Let's do it one more time."

Teddy-as-Mark reset to his spot. When Peter called "Action," he walked nervously into the frame.

Right on cue, the door of the building he was passing flew open and Logan rushed out. Upon seeing him, Teddy dashed out of the frame.

"Hey! Storm! Where the hell do you think you're going?" Logan yelled, then raced after him.

"Cut." Peter took a step away from the monitor, beaming. "That's the take. Good job, gentlemen. Mark, I believe that's all we need you for today."

Teddy thanked the crew before making his way to his trailer. As he started to change himself into Billy Barnett, his phone rang with a call from Mori.

"Rebecca's car has been found," the lawyer said.

"Where?"

"An impound yard. Apparently, it had been left in a grocery store parking lot for over a day, so they had it towed. Carl is going to send someone to pick it up."

"Tell him not to do that until I say it's okay. My contact will want to check it before anyone else gets their fingerprints all over it. Text me the address and I'll forward it to him."

Instead of transforming back into Billy, Teddy donned his Detective Thompson disguise, and then slipped off the set unseen.

When he reached the production sedan he was using, he found a flyer sticking out from under its window wiper and pulled it free. On it was a picture of a young man, with MISSING: JUSTIN ROGERS printed below it. According to the flyer, Justin had last been seen the day before, near where **Storm's Eye** had been shooting. He had not been heard from since.

Teddy guessed the flyer was the work of concerned friends or family. He studied the picture for a moment, but didn't recognize Justin, so he set the paper on his passenger seat to throw away later.

His first stop was at the grocery store where Rebecca's Mercedes had been left. He talked to the manager who'd had it towed, but all the woman knew was that the vehicle had been there at least a day when she'd made the call. Neither she nor any of her employees had seen anyone near it.

Teddy went to the impound yard next.

A flash of his police badge earned him a quick escort to Rebecca's car.

He walked around the vehicle, looking for dents or scratches or scuff marks that might have come from a struggle when Rebecca was taken. But he found none.

He went over every inch of the car's interior, looking for fingerprints and anything that could aid him in finding the kidnappers. Unfortunately, whoever had ditched the car had done a thorough job of cleaning it first. Which was a clue in itself—the kidnappers weren't mere opportunists but experienced criminals.

He texted Mori that someone could pick up the car and left.

26

AT FIVE P.M., THE CAST AND MUCH OF THE CREW were released for the day. Those who remained would be shooting B-roll of the street and the buildings surrounding it.

Stacy, who had joined the others in the cast seating area for the last few shots, hopped out of her chair and looked at Matthew. "Free tonight?"

"Me? Yes, I'm free. Why?"

"Adriene and I are having dinner at the hotel in about an hour, why don't you join us?"

While it wouldn't be as good as eating with Tessa, it would be a great excuse to be at the hotel and to ingratiate himself further within the group. "If you're sure I wouldn't be imposing."

"Not at all. At the very least, we owe you a meal."

"You don't owe me anything."

"You say that, but it's not true."

He curled his lips into a shy smile. He was getting very good at playing the reluctant hero. "Sure. I'd love to join you."

"Great. Meet us in the lobby in an hour."

When Matthew reached his car, he found a flyer on his windshield. Without even looking at it, he crumpled it up and threw it onto the ground, then climbed inside and headed to the hotel.

27

KORDO SIPPED FROM HIS GLASS OF BEER AND EYED the lobby of the Santa Barbara Hills Hotel. From his table at the bar, he could see all the way to the hotel entrance. He had spent most of the day on the set, but when Barnett failed to show up, he'd decided to switch tactics and watch for him at the hotel.

Though plenty of people moved in and out, Barnett had yet to make an appearance there, either. But unlike on the set, Kordo was sure he'd show up soon. It was nearing dinnertime, and everyone knew those Hollywood types always liked to dress up and go out for glamorous meals.

All Kordo needed to do was wait.

◆ ◆ ◆

MATTHEW ARRIVED AT THE SANTA BARBARA HILLS
Hotel a full twenty minutes before he was to
meet Stacy and Adriene. To kill time, he took a
seat at the bar.

The bartender, a woman about his age, walked
over. "What can I get you?"

"Martini, please." Matthew had read in an
interview that Tessa liked them, so they had become his go-to drink.

While he waited for it to arrive, his gaze
drifted across the bar area. He'd registered the
man sitting at the table when he'd walked in but
hadn't paid attention to him until now.

It was the fake guard from the set, only now
instead of wearing a security outfit, he was
dressed in a suit. He seemed particularly interested in what was going on in the lobby.

"Here you are, sir." The bartender set a martini in front of Matthew and left to help another
customer.

Matthew took a sip and looked back at the
man at the table, intrigued.

28

TEDDY WAS IN BILLY'S SUITE, HAVING RETURNED TO the hotel ten minutes before Kordo took a seat in the bar.

After taking a shower to wash away his detective disguise, he checked the time. He needed to hurry if he was going to make it to the Novaks' house by six p.m. If he was right, another video would arrive around that time. He wanted to be there when it did.

He changed himself into Billy Barnett and headed downstairs. As he crossed the hotel lobby, he once more felt eyes watching him. This time, though, he sensed it was more than just a fan looking his way.

Casually, he scanned the room. As his gaze

reached the bar, a man at a table near its entrance looked away.

Perhaps it was coincidence, perhaps not. Teddy couldn't get a solid read on the guy. He did notice Matthew was also at the bar, though the kid didn't seem to realize Teddy was there.

If Teddy hadn't been pressed for time, he would have made a more thorough search. He headed outside and the valet brought him his Porsche.

As Teddy climbed into his car, the feeling of being watched returned. He glanced back through the glass doors into the hotel lobby.

The same guy who'd been sitting at the table in the bar now stood several feet away inside, talking on a phone and trying very hard to act like he wasn't looking at Teddy.

Maybe he **was** a film fan. That kind of attention was something that occurred more when Teddy was Mark Weldon than Billy Barnett, but it did happen.

He noted the man's features in case he saw him again, then put his Porsche in gear.

INSIDE THE LOBBY, KORDO WATCHED BARNETT PULL away. "He's leaving now," he said into his phone. "I need to go."

"No," Neno said. "If you follow him, you might lose him again."

The words stung. "But I thought you wanted me to—"

"Stay there until I call you back. I'll find out what room he's in, then you can wait there until he comes back."

29

MATTHEW TOOK ANOTHER SIP OF HIS MARTINI AS HE
watched the faux guard walk across the lobby
toward the hotel entrance. The man stopped a
dozen feet from the doors and made a phone call.
When he hung up, he sat on one of the lobby
chairs.

"Huh," Matthew said under his breath. The
guy had clearly been watching Billy Barnett.
But why?

Over the next several minutes, the man
switched back and forth from checking his phone
to looking out the glass doors. Finally, whatever
message he'd been waiting for arrived. After reading it, he headed to the elevators.

Matthew knew it wasn't his business, but cu-
riosity got the better of him. Besides, he still had

some time until dinner. He dropped some cash on the bar and followed the man.

When he reached the elevator waiting area, the doors of the car the man had entered had already closed.

Matthew pushed the call button. While he waited, he watched the floor indicator for the faux guard's elevator. It stopped on the fourth floor, then started down again.

That was interesting.

Matthew had used a stolen master keycard to sneak into housekeeping when no one was there and obtained a list of guests and the rooms they were in. So he knew the fourth floor was where Tessa, Peter Barrington, Mark Weldon, and Billy Barnett were staying. And now Ben Bacchetti, too, he reminded himself.

The door of another elevator car opened. Matthew hesitated. He probably should forget about the man and go back to the bar. But before the doors closed, he slipped inside and pressed the button for four.

When he arrived, the hallway was empty.

If the guy was still here, he had to be in one of the rooms. And given the man's interest in Billy, the producer's suite seemed the smart bet.

Matthew moved quietly down the corridor. When he reached Billy's door, he leaned close and listened.

Someone was moving around inside. He had seen Billy leave, so it had to be the faux guard breaking in.

This could be another opportunity for him to play the hero, Matthew realized. An opportunity from which he could gain the appreciation of Billy Barnett himself, a close personal friend of Tessa's. Having him in Matthew's corner would only help to smooth Matthew's path to permanently being by her side, wouldn't it?

Matthew retrieved the master keycard and tapped it against the card reader.

SINCE KORDO HAD SOME TIME TO KILL BEFORE Barnett returned, he decided to search the room for anything that might explain why a movie producer would be involved in the search for Rebecca Novak. He went into the bedroom and checked the closet and the dresser but found nothing but clothes.

On the floor next to the dresser was a suitcase. He grabbed it and was about to swing it onto the bed when he heard the front-door lock click.

Barnett must have forgotten something and come back.

Kordo hurried into the living room, planning to yank Barnett inside and incapacitate him.

Only when the door opened, it wasn't Barnett on the other side, it was the guy from the movie set. The one Kordo had noticed glancing at him.

"I think you're in the wrong place, buddy," the man said. "Because, unless you're a master of disguise, you're not Billy Barnett."

Kordo pulled the door out of the way, then punched the guy in the gut, doubling him over and sending him stumbling into the doorframe.

Kordo grabbed the man's shoulders. "You should stay out of things not your business." He then kneed the guy in the face and pushed him to the floor. "You make big mistake."

Kordo grabbed the door and tried to shove it closed, but the guy's legs were in the way.

Kordo grunted in frustration, then reached into his jacket and wrapped his fingers around the grip of his gun, intending to put a quick end to the troublemaker. But before he could pull his weapon out, he heard the door of a nearby room open and voices in the hall.

He cursed.

No way he could kill the asshole and pull him into the room before someone walked by.

He jerked the door open and raced into the hallway.

30

MOMENTS BEFORE, TESSA WAS PUTTING ON HER earrings and checking herself in the mirror.

Perfect, she thought.

She turned to tell Ben she was ready to go, when something thumped against the wall.

Ben looked up from his laptop. "What was that?"

"I don't know. But I think it came from Billy's suite."

Another bang against the wall caused them both to jump up and run for the door.

Ben exited the room first, with Tessa hot on his heels. As they entered the corridor, a man raced out of Billy's suite and sprinted in the other direction.

"Hey! Stop!" Ben yelled.

The man ignored him. When he reached a door marked STAIRS, he shoved it open and disappeared inside.

A low moan drifted into the hall from Billy's suite.

Tessa and Ben hurried to the doorway.

A man lay across the threshold, his legs keeping the door from closing.

Tessa pushed the door out of the way and knelt beside him. "It's Matthew."

"Matthew?" Ben looked confused, then his eyes widened. "The kid who helped Adriene and Stacy."

"Yes. Call 911."

While Ben dialed, Tessa fetched a damp towel from Billy's bathroom, and wiped away the blood dripping from the corner of Matthew's mouth.

"An ambulance is on the way," Ben said.

Matthew groaned again and then blinked. "What? Why am I—" He blinked again. "Tessa?"

"It's okay. You're going to be fine."

Matthew tensed. "There's a guy in Mr. Barnett's room."

"He ran off," Ben said. "Do you know who he was?"

When Matthew tried to shake his head, he winced in pain. "I noticed him spying on Mr. Barnett downstairs. When Mr. Barnett left, he came up here, so I followed him. The door was propped open. Maybe I shouldn't have, but I looked inside. That's when he attacked me."

"Let's not worry about that right now," Tessa said. "You need to rest. The paramedics will be here soon."

Despite the pain he was feeling, Matthew struggled to keep the smile from his face. His hope had been that confronting the suspicious man would ingratiate him with Billy. He had never considered the possibility that his actions would result directly in Tessa comforting him.

Still, best he not look weak in front of her. "I'm . . . I'm okay."

"Maybe you should look at yourself in a mirror before you say that. Just relax. I'm here with you."

His heart fluttered. "Thank you."

31

EVENING TRAFFIC KEPT TEDDY FROM REACHING THE
Novaks' mansion until a quarter after six.

Vulin ushered him into the library, where
Novak and Mori waited.

"Did a new video arrive?"

Mori nodded. "We think so."

"'Think so'?"

"Carl found this on his office desk a few minutes ago." Mori held up a small plastic bag. Inside
was a thumb drive.

"I've never seen it before," Novak said. "And it
wasn't there a half hour ago."

"Have you tried to see what's on it?"

"I thought it better if we waited for you,"
Mori said.

The lawyer opened his laptop, then unzipped the bag.

Teddy held up his palm. "Hold on. Has anyone touched the drive?"

A nod from Novak. "I did, but only once."

Teddy looked at Mori, who shook his head.

"I scooted it back into the bag with a pen."

"Good. Let me take it out."

Holding on to the drive through the plastic, Teddy eased the connector end out and plugged it into the port on the computer. An icon appeared on the screen. Teddy clicked it.

The thumb drive contained a single video file. He opened it and clicked PLAY.

Like yesterday's video, Rebecca was once again sitting on the cot. The only differences were that the number on the wall had been changed to a three, and one of her cheeks was redder than the other.

Novak stared at the screen. "Mr. Barnett, we've got to find her. Now."

"My contact is making progress."

"What does that mean?"

"It means he's doing everything he or anyone else can do to find her."

"But what if it's not enough?"

Teddy's phone buzzed with a text from Ben Bacchetti.

Call me ASAP.

"I understand your concern. But my friend is your best chance at freeing her. I need to make a call. Excuse me for a moment."

He stepped into the hallway and called Ben.

"What is it?"

"Apparently, someone has been keeping tabs on you. When you left, he broke into your room. Matthew stopped him before he could do much, though."

"Matthew who?"

"Matthew Wagner. Stacy's new friend."

"What was he doing there?"

"He was in the bar when he noticed a guy watching you when you left and followed him up to your suite."

"Which suite?"

"Billy's."

"Matthew must be bucking for a role in our next superhero movie."

"We don't do superhero movies."

"Someone should tell him that."

"The police want to talk to you."

"Are they there now?"

"Yes."

"Tell them I'll be back as soon as I can."

♦ ♦ ♦

"I WASN'T HERE," TEDDY SAID. "AND I HAVE NO IDEA who would want to break into my room. Sorry. I wish I could be of more help."

"If you think of someone, we'd appreciate you letting us know." The officer handed Teddy a business card.

"When can I get back into my room?"

"Let me check with our tech. I think he's almost done." The officer disappeared inside the suite, then returned a minute later with the crime scene tech in tow. "It's all yours. Again, call us if you think of anyone."

"I will."

Teddy entered his suite, expecting the place to be a disaster. What he found, though, were a few dresser drawers hanging open and some clothes moved around, but that was it. It appeared Matthew's intervention had stopped the intruder from finding anything of interest.

Teddy retrieved his laptop from where he kept it hidden under the living room bar. He logged onto the Santa Barbara Hills Hotel's security system and accessed the stored video. Hacking into the system had been one of the first things he'd done after checking into the hotel. He hadn't expected trouble, but years of experience had taught him to prepare for anything.

It didn't take him long to discover that the intruder must have been carrying a jamming device. Anytime the guy came within twenty feet of a camera, the video degraded to static.

Teddy was able to pull a semi-decent shot of the man from footage taken in the hotel lobby, though. It was good enough for him to positively identify the intruder as the man who'd been sitting at the bar when Teddy left earlier.

Clicking through the video, Teddy followed Matthew up to the suite. For the most part, it confirmed Matthew's story. The only discrepancy occurred in the hall outside Teddy's room.

The doors to the rooms at the Santa Barbara Hills Hotel were inset a good foot into the hallway walls. So, while the camera could see the entrance to the suite, the door itself was hidden from view.

According to Ben, Matthew said the door had been ajar, and he'd only needed to push it to enter the room. On the video, however, Matthew not only took longer at the door than Teddy expected, but he also removed something from his pocket prior to going inside. Perhaps the item was something Matthew thought he could use as a weapon. If Teddy saw him again, he'd ask.

From a secret compartment in his makeup case, Teddy retrieved a latent fingerprint kit, then searched his rooms for any prints the intruder might have left. The man must have been wearing gloves, though, because the only prints Teddy found were his own.

Whoever the intruder was and why he had wanted to search Teddy's rooms were questions Teddy couldn't answer. Not yet anyway. So he returned his focus to Rebecca's kidnapping.

He retrieved the bag containing the thumb drive Novak had received, dusted it, and found four distinct prints.

Though it had been some time since Teddy had parted ways with the CIA, he still had a back door into its network. He uploaded the prints to it and started running them through the databases the Agency had access to.

While he waited for the results, he checked his email. As always, there were a lot of messages.

Among them was one from the film's associate producer in charge of postproduction. She sent the same basic email every night containing links to footage of what had been shot that day. This included both what Peter was shooting for the film and behind-the-scenes footage for promotional purposes.

According to what Matthew told Ben, the intruder had been posing as a guard on set that day. It took Teddy only a few minutes of scrolling through the behind-the-scenes footage to find shots of him. They were much better images than the one the security camera caught in the hotel lobby.

After capturing several screenshots, he connected back to the CIA server and uploaded the clearest picture of the man to the facial recognition search engine. He then checked to see if there had been any hits on the fingerprints.

As he'd suspected, two of the prints belonged to Carl Novak. The other two did not, however. But they did belong to someone whose prints were on file with the Citizenship and Immigration Service.

"Well, well, well."

32

"WAIT HERE UNTIL I GIVE YOU THE OKAY," TEDDY whispered, then crept across the dark room.

His hair was slicked back, and he had a scar on his cheek that peeked out from under the sunglasses he wore, even though it was night. They were part of the look he'd created for Billy's fictional "contact."

When he reached the sleeping form on the bed, he grabbed the man's shoulder and gave it a hard shove.

"Rise and shine, Mr. Vulin."

The Novaks' estate manager's eyes popped open as he jolted awake. At the sight of Teddy looming over him, he jerked again.

The first words he sputtered were in what Teddy assumed was Croatian. Realizing his mistake, Vulin switched to English. "Who are you? What are you doing in my room?"

"I believe you left this behind." Teddy dangled the clear plastic bag that contained the thumb drive in front of his face.

"What do you mean? That—that's not mine."

"I never said it was. But you did deliver it."

"Deliver? Are you crazy? I've never seen that thing before."

"That's odd. Then how did your fingerprints get on it?"

Vulin blanched.

"What we'd like to know is: Who gave it to you?"

The man's brow furrowed, then his gaze flicked to the darkness behind Teddy. "'We'?"

Without taking his eyes off Vulin, Teddy said, "Lights."

A lamp on the dresser came on, revealing Novak and Mori.

What was left of Vulin's defenses crumbled. "Mr. Novak. Oh, God. I'm sorry. I'm so sorry."

Novak fought to keep his expression neutral as he and Mori joined Teddy at the bed. "Tell him what he wants to know, Andrew."

"I didn't want to do it, but . . ."

"But you did," Teddy said.

Vulin squeezed his eyes shut and nodded. "I had no choice."

"Who gave it to you?"

Teddy let the silence that followed linger, knowing Vulin would soon realize he had no other option but to tell them the truth. "Zoran Janic."

Novak stiffened, then in a halting voice said, "Zoran Janic? He's who took Rebecca?"

"He's behind it, but I don't think he's here in the States. One of his men gave the drive to me."

"Then how do you know Janic's involved?" Teddy asked.

"He made the initial contact with me."

"When?"

"A few weeks ago."

"And he asked you to leave notes and cause the problems for the Novaks?" Teddy questioned.

"Not asked. Ordered."

Anger flared in Novak's eyes. "Why? Why would you even listen to him? Have we not been good to you?"

"You have. You've been more than good. But he . . . he's holding my brother and his family. He told me he'd kill them if I didn't do as he said."

Novak blinked, stunned again.

"Did you know he was going to kidnap Mrs. Novak?" Teddy asked.

Vulin shook his head adamantly. "I had no idea. If I'd known . . ." He turned back to Novak. "I'm so sorry. You can do anything you want to me, but my brother and his wife, my nieces.

They're innocent. Don't let them die because of what I did." He grabbed Novak's hand. "Please. He'll kill them."

It took a moment for Novak's shock to subside. When it did, he pulled his hand free and took a step away from the bed. Vulin kept his eyes on him, wordlessly pleading his case.

Teddy snapped his fingers to get Vulin's attention. "When did you put the drive on Mr. Novak's desk?"

"Six oh seven p.m. That's when I was told to do it."

"Six oh seven precisely?"

"Yes."

"By Janic?"

"No. By the man who gave it to me."

"Describe him for me."

Teddy assumed Vulin would describe the man who'd broken into his suite, but the guy Vulin had talked to was not the same. Vulin's contact was balding and had a broad face. The man from Teddy's suite had hair almost long enough to pull into a ponytail, and his face was narrow, almost gaunt. So, definitely not Teddy's intruder. But the description did bring to mind someone else.

Teddy pulled out his phone, brought up a picture, and showed it to Vulin.

"Yes. That's him. That's the man."

Teddy turned the screen so Novak and Mori could see. The picture was the enhanced still of

Rebecca's car leaving the flower shop. The man who'd given Vulin the thumb drive was the same man who'd driven the Mercedes away.

"Stay here," Teddy told Vulin. "Your room and the rest of the house is being watched. If you try to run, you won't get far."

"Where would I go?"

Teddy motioned for Novak and Mori to follow him out of the room. He didn't say a word until they were behind the closed doors of Novak's library.

"I assume Zoran Janic's related to the Leon Janic you mentioned before?"

"He's Leon's older brother."

"Why would your friend's brother want to kidnap your wife?"

Novak slumped onto one of the couches, his head falling into his hands. "Because he thinks I killed Leon."

"Why is that?"

"Leon and Zoran were nothing alike. Zoran is vicious and mean, has been from birth. He was already in a gang when I met Leon. He loved to brag about the people he beat up, about the money he'd forced others to give him. Leon was nice and funny and kind. They were almost complete opposites, but despite how different they were, they loved each other.

"One trait they did have in common was that neither was afraid of anything. Leon pushed me to try things I would have never done on my own. He taught me how to take risks. In a way, he's more responsible for the man I've become than anyone else. But his fearlessness was also his downfall."

Novak rubbed his temple. "One day, Leon talked me into exploring the ruins of an old factory. The place had been heavily damaged during the war. The area was off-limits for good reason, but we were young and stupid."

He started to say something, then had to stop as his eyes filled with tears. It took another few moments before he was able to go on. "Leon stepped on a land mine that should have been removed but hadn't. He survived the explosion but was in a coma for five days." He looked at Teddy. "At 6:07 p.m. on the fifth day, he took his last breath."

That solved the mystery of why the messages were arriving when they did.

"I still don't understand why Zoran blames you."

"He believed—still believes, I guess—that it was my idea to go to the ruins. That Leon would never have been so stupid. He almost killed me back then. Would have if others hadn't stopped him. He vowed to make me pay. To protect me, my parents sent me to live with my aunt and uncle in London. Zoran hasn't tried anything in all the years since then. I had thought he'd come to his senses or, at the very least, forgotten about me. But I guess he was only biding his time."

He stared at the floor, then nodded to himself and looked at Teddy again. "I need to ask for another favor. Is that something I should talk to Mr. Barnett about?"

"He'd only call me, so go ahead."

"Andrew has been a trusted member of my staff for years. He is . . . he is a friend. I may be furious with him right now, but I understand why he did what he did. I don't want his family to die because of my problems with Zoran Janic."

"Are you asking me to save them?"

"Yes."

"You realize I can't be in two places at one time."

"I thought that perhaps a man such as yourself would know others who might be able to help. Please. I'll pay whatever it costs."

"I can't promise you anything. But I'll look into it."

"Thank you."

33

AFTER TEDDY ARRIVED BACK AT HIS SUITE, HE CALLED
an old friend.

"This can't be who I think it is." Vesna Martic's
tone was both amused and surprised. A former
Bosnian intelligence operative, she and Teddy
had worked together many times when he'd still
been in the CIA.

"That depends on who you think it is."

"Word on the street is that you're dead."

"Consider this a call from the afterlife, then."

"I hope you're not reversing the charges."

"You do still owe me for that little scrape I got
you out of last time I saw you."

"Which was payback for me keeping you out
of prison the time before that."

"Why, Vesna, I have no idea what you're talk-ing about."

"Of course you don't." She snorted a laugh. "You're going to ask me for another one of your favors, aren't you? One that you'll conveniently forget about later?"

"Yes, a favor. But it's large enough I don't think I'll be able to forget it."

"Why do I have the sudden urge to hang up?"

"How's your knowledge of Balkan area crime syndicates?"

"Better than most."

"Then I'm guessing you know who Zoran Janic is."

Her tone turned icy. "If you're asking me to do something for him, I'll end this conversation right now."

"Not for him. **To** him."

Silence, then, "I'm listening."

34

THE NEXT MORNING, TEDDY CHECKED THE FACIAL recognition search he'd started running last night. When he'd taken a look before falling asleep, there had been no results. This time, however, he had a potential match.

The second he saw the person's picture, he knew he'd found the identity of his intruder. The man looking back at him was identical to the man in the security footage.

The match's name was Sava Kordo. He had a long arrest record and outstanding warrants from several European countries, but had never been convicted.

He was also a known associate of the Janic crime family.

Bingo.

Kordo had to be involved in Rebecca's kid-napping, and had likely targeted Billy Barnett because Billy had met with Novak and Mori.

If Teddy could find him, he was sure Kordo would lead him right to Rebecca.

He texted the picture and info to Mike Freeman and followed up with a call.

"Get the photo to your men at the set. I don't think this guy will try to show up dressed as a security guard again, but I'm betting he'll be in the area."

"What do you want them to do if they find him?"

"Contact me right away, but do not engage. I don't want him to know he's been seen."

"Consider it done."

35

KORDO SAT IN HIS CAR DOWN THE STREET FROM THE production trucks for **Storm's Eye.** Filming had moved from yesterday's downtown location to the exterior of a café a block from the beach.

Thanks to his encounter with that nosy jerk at the hotel last night, sneaking onto the set in his guard uniform was no longer an option.

He could work around that. All he needed to do was to find Barnett's Porsche. Once he did, he would follow Barnett when he left, and deal with the producer someplace quieter.

A woman approached his car and started to put a piece of paper under his windshield wiper.

He tapped the glass and scowled, causing her to jump and grab her chest. "Sorry, I didn't see you."

When he didn't respond, she motioned for him to open his window. Kordo waved for her to move on, but she remained where she was.

With a roll of his eyes, he lowered the window halfway. "What?"

She held out the piece of paper. "We're looking for a friend of ours who's gone missing. Maybe you've seen him?"

"I haven't. Sorry."

"You didn't even look at his picture."

Hoping it would make her go away, he snatched the flyer and glanced at it. He shook his head. "Like I said, I do not know him."

When he tried to give the flyer back, the woman took a step away.

"Keep it. Maybe you'll see him later. If you do, call the number. Thanks."

As she hurried to the next parked car, Kordo crumpled the flyer and tossed it into the back seat.

DANIEL RIVERA WAS MIKE FREEMAN'S TOP SECURITY man at the West Coast offices of Strategic Services. That was why he was now in charge of security on the set of **Storm's Eye.**

Not only did he have everyone on high alert, but he and several of his people were roaming the area around the shoot, keeping an eye out for Kordo.

Rivera was starting to think the guy wasn't going to show up when his radio hissed to life. "Kwon for Rivera."

"Go for Rivera."

"I've got eyes on a man sitting in a car, a block and a half from the north end of the set. He fits the description."

"Keep him in sight, but do not approach. I repeat, do not approach."

"Copy."

Rivera pushed the TALK button again. "Rivera for Hansen."

"Go for Hansen."

"Are you in your car yet?"

"Yes."

"You heard Kwon?"

"I did."

"If the guy runs, you know what to do."

"Follow."

Rivera exchanged his radio for his phone and called Billy Barnett.

KORDO GRIMACED AS THE SKIN ON THE BACK OF HIS neck continued to tingle.

For the past three minutes, he'd been watching a man loitering at the corner, about a half block away. Like on the other shoot days, there were plenty of fans milling about. Someone hanging around the area in and of itself wasn't a concern.

The thing that had triggered Kordo's internal alarm was that on at least four occasions, the guy had glanced in Kordo's direction. The man may have been waiting for a friend, but Kordo had enough experience to know not to count on that.

Which was why he decided it was time to get out of there.

"THIS IS KWON. HE'S LEAVING."

"Copy. Hansen?"

"Moving out now."

NENO CHECKED HIS WATCH. WHERE THE HELL WAS Kordo? He'd promised to come back by lunchtime to help record today's video. He should have been here an hour ago.

As he reached for his phone, it started ringing, and Kordo's name appeared on the caller ID.

Finally.

Neno punched ACCEPT. "You'd better be calling me to say you're almost here."

"I'm being followed."

"Followed? By who?"

"Not sure. Someone from the movie crew, I think."

"How do they even know—" Neno stopped himself. There would be time for questions later. "Lose him, then find someplace to lay low. Do not come back here. There might be another tail you haven't seen yet."

"I would know."

"Your history doesn't back you up."

Kordo said nothing.

"Do not come back until I give you the okay. Understand?"

"Yeah, yeah. I understand."

TEDDY SPENT THE MORNING SEARCHING HOTEL parking lots for the car that had followed him the evening after Rebecca's kidnapping. If he was right, it had been driven by either Kordo or the broad-faced man. By the time Rivera called him, he was already halfway across town.

He raced toward the set but was still a mile away when Rivera called again.

"He just left. I think he got spooked. But I have a man following him."

"Can you conference him in?"

A couple of moments later, Hansen joined the call.

"Where are you?" Teddy asked.

"On the 101 freeway, southbound."

"Does he know you're following him?"

"From the way he's driving, I'm pretty sure he does."

That was unfortunate, but they couldn't do anything about it now. "Keep me posted on any changes. I'm heading your way."

36

KORDO SPED SOUTH ON THE FREEWAY, OUT OF Santa Barbara and past Montecito and Summerland. He'd been hoping to lose his tail in the traffic, but the other driver knew what he was doing.

Kordo needed to try something different.

He spotted a sign for an upcoming exit to a town called Carpinteria. Hopefully, it would be big enough to get lost in. He waited until the last moment, then flew across the lanes and raced down the exit ramp.

When he looked into his rearview mirror, he saw that the other car was still behind him.

"Dammit."

He rolled through the stop at the bottom of the ramp, turned right, and gunned the engine.

The town didn't appear to be as large as Santa Barbara but looked big enough for his purposes.

He drove into a residential area and began taking random turns.

The guy behind him was good, but not good enough. After several minutes, Kordo was finally free of him.

TEDDY TOOK THE CARPINTERIA OFF-RAMP AND called Hansen.

"Update?"

"I'm sorry, Mr. Barnett. I lost him about a minute ago."

"Where?"

Hansen told him the last place he'd seen Kordo's car.

"He can't have gone far," Teddy said. "Go back to the freeway and make sure he doesn't get on it again. I'll look around."

AFTER HIDING IN A QUIET NEIGHBORHOOD FOR several minutes, Kordo used his phone's GPS to find the quickest way back to the freeway.

As he headed toward the main road, he spotted a very distinctive car pass through the upcoming intersection.

It couldn't be, could it?

He raced to the corner and turned left. The other car was already a block ahead, but there was no mistaking its shape. It was a classic 1958 Porsche 356 Speedster. The same type of car Billy Barnett drove.

Kordo grabbed his binoculars and checked the Porsche's license plate.

He laughed.

The man he'd been looking for was right in front of him. Kordo didn't believe for a second that Barnett's presence in Carpinteria was coincidence. The person who'd been following him must have called the producer and Barnett had come running.

It was as if the universe had delivered Barnett to Kordo on a silver platter. There was no way he was going to refuse the gift.

Kordo closed the gap between them to a half block, then took the next left fast enough so that his tires squealed on the road, sure that the sound would draw Barnett's attention. He then kept going straight, an eye on his mirror.

He was almost to the next intersection when the Porsche rounded the corner behind him.

With a smile, he reached under his jacket and released the safety strap holding his gun in his shoulder holster.

Now, all he needed was someplace quiet. He brought up the GPS again and searched for the perfect spot. It didn't take long to find one.

The only potential problem was the guy who had followed him from Santa Barbara. It was possible he was watching the freeway, hoping to block Kordo's escape. That's what Kordo would have done.

To avoid him, Kordo chose a route that went under the freeway a half mile to the north of the 101 entrance.

As he drove, he glanced at his mirror every few seconds to confirm Barnett was still behind him. The Porsche was always there, always maintaining a consistent block-long gap between them.

When Kordo reached the hills east of town, he turned left onto a two-lane road that wound up the side of a mountain.

He kept an eye out for someplace he could flip the table on Barnett. A road that turned off into a canyon would do. Even a turnout where he could stop and let Barnett either race by or pull in behind him would be enough.

At the moment, however, the road was pinned in on the left by the upward slope of the mountain, and on the right by a steep drop-off.

As he cornered the next bend, he caught a glimpse ahead of the road going around another ridge. He'd only been able to see it for a second or two, but he was sure he spotted a turnout that would work.

He glanced at the mirror again and watched the Porsche come around the turn behind him.

With a grin, he looked back at the road, then gasped. The next turn loomed directly in front of him, much closer than he'd expected.

He hit the brakes and yanked the steering wheel to the right. The tires fought to maintain contact with the road, and his sedan swerved into the oncoming lane. If there'd been a car coming the other way, they'd both have been splattered all over the side of the mountain.

His car swung back into the uphill lane, but Kordo's troubles weren't over yet. Less than a hundred feet ahead, the road curved in the other direction.

He fought the wheel again and swore at his sedan to stay on the asphalt.

The tires screamed as they skidded sideways toward the narrow shoulder.

"Hold on," he growled.

There was a **thunk** as the tires on the passenger side slipped off the road and onto the dirt, sending a cloud of dust billowing into the air.

Then all noise vanished as his car flew over the side and plunged down the mountain.

37

TEDDY'S SPEED WASN'T MUCH SLOWER THAN THAT of Kordo's sedan. The difference was that his Porsche was a high-performance vehicle designed to take turns fast, while Kordo's was not.

Teddy watched as the other car barely made it through the upcoming turn. When the road curved again, the car fought once more to stay in its lane, but the forces working against it were too great.

In a puff of dust, it disappeared over the side.

Billy pulled onto the narrow shoulder just past where the sedan had gone over and jumped out.

A pickup truck that had been coming down the mountain joined him a moment later. Its driver, a man in his early twenties, hurried over to where Teddy was peering down the mountainside. "Oh, my God. Did you see that?"

Kordo's car lay on its roof about a hundred feet below. Thankfully, the slope was not as steep here as it was a little farther up, or else the vehicle would have still been rolling downhill.

Teddy glanced at the other man. "Call 911. I'll see if I can help him."

"Dude, maybe I should do it."

"I've got it. You make the call."

"Okay, but wait a sec." The guy ran back to his pickup and returned a moment later with a first-aid kit. "Take this."

Teddy grabbed the kit and started down the slope. The front of the sedan was pointed uphill. This allowed him to approach the driver's-side window without worrying that the car might tumble onto him.

Kordo hung upside down in his seat, his arms dangling toward the roof. Blood dripped down his neck and off his forehead.

Teddy reached through the broken window and checked the man's pulse, then cursed.

The first-aid kit was unnecessary.

Teddy had needed Kordo alive. He had been the best chance to find out where Rebecca was being held. Hopefully, the guy had a phone. If so, then at least all might not be lost.

Teddy reached into the car again and searched the dead man.

Kordo had a gun hanging halfway out of a shoulder holster, and what felt like some money in a pocket of his pants. Teddy left both where they were.

He turned on the flashlight of his phone and shined it into the car. It didn't take long to spot the glass face of a phone, lying on the roof, half covered by a crumpled piece of paper.

Teddy leaned through the window and grabbed both the phone and the paper. The phone was still working, but the screen was locked. As for the paper, it was one of those missing-person flyers Teddy had seen all day. Yet more proof that the guy had been hanging around the set.

Teddy held the phone in front of Kordo to try to unlock it, hoping the lacerations on the man's face wouldn't hinder the facial recognition software. But the phone remained closed. He'd worry about that problem later.

After stuffing the phone in his pocket, he took a step away from the car.

"How is he?" a voice from above called.

Teddy glanced up the slope. The driver who'd stopped earlier had been joined by three others. Teddy shook his head and started the slow climb back to the road.

By the time he reached the top, two Santa Barbara County sheriff vehicles had arrived.

"How many people in the car?" one of the deputies asked.

"Only the driver. He's dead."

"Is that your Porsche, sir?"

"It is. I saw him go over the side, so I stopped to see if I could help."

"We need you to come down to the station."

"Me? Why?"

"We had a report of two vehicles racing up this road. The description of one matches your car. The other matches the one down there."

"There was no racing as far as I know, but if you need me at the station, I'm happy to help out."

THE FIRST THING TEDDY DID UPON ARRIVING AT THE sheriff's station was to call Stone and explain his current predicament.

"So what you're saying is you need me to bust you out of jail?"

"Technically, I haven't been put behind bars yet, but that's basically the idea."

"Let me see if I can pull a few strings. Until then, try to be a model prisoner."

"I feel it's worth repeating, I'm not a prisoner yet."

"Right. Lucky for you, I'll be in Santa Barbara tonight. If my contacts don't work out, I'll bring you a cake with a file in it."

"I would expect nothing less."

Thirty minutes later, Teddy was thanked and told he could leave.

38

WHILE REBECCA HAD NO WAY OF TELLING THE ACTUAL time, she was getting good at knowing when her meals would arrive.

Only a few minutes after she'd pressed her ear against the door, she heard footsteps in the hallway outside, heading her way.

She waited until they neared, then rushed to the cot and sat down.

A moment later, the steps stopped on the other side of the door and the lock turned.

The man who entered the room was the taller, wider one. He carried a paper bag in one hand and a can of soda in the other. Like always, he wore a white mask. Behind him was the shortest of the group, also masked. He remained in the hallway, as he often did, no doubt as a deterrent in case she tried to bolt out the door.

The face coverings made them look like low-rent serial killers in a bad horror movie. The thought was so humorous, she almost laughed out loud but refrained. She knew doing so would be a mistake.

The oaf lumbered over to her table and set the bag and soda on it. She could smell the now all-too-familiar odor of reheated hamburger.

As he placed the food down, the guy looked at her, his dark eyes staring at her through the holes in his mask.

No, not staring. Leering.

Her skin began to crawl, but she kept her face neutral, not wanting to give him the satisfaction of knowing he was getting to her.

"Eat," he said.

A real wordsmith, this one. She'd never heard him say more than one word at a time. She guessed that his English was a lot worse than his buddies'.

When she made no move for the bag, he tilted his head, his eyes never leaving hers. "Eat."

"I'm not hungry."

His hand shot out so fast, she almost didn't see it. Instead of grabbing her, though, he stopped it less than an inch from her arm. His fingers hovered over her skin, sending a new wave of revulsion through her. Then, slowly, he moved one finger down her arm, as if tracing the bones beneath.

"Not eat. Can do . . ." He paused, searching for words. ". . . other thing." It was the most he'd ever said at one time, and she would have given anything not to hear any of it.

She tried to pull her arm away, but he followed it, his finger never losing contact with her.

The man in the hallway leaned through the doorway, as if trying to see what was happening. He then barked something Rebecca didn't understand. The oaf stiffened, then with obvious reluctance pulled his hand away.

The short one shouted something again, clearly not happy with his friend.

The oaf took a step back. His gaze stayed on Rebecca until he finally turned and exited the room.

When the door shut and she was alone again, she exhaled a breath she'd been holding for far too long.

She looked at the door, her eyes narrowing to angry slits.

No matter what happened, she would not let them break her.

39

EARLY THAT AFTERNOON, MATTHEW PARKED DOWN
the street from the Santa Barbara Hills Hotel and
checked himself in his mirror. Last night's one-
sided fight against Billy's intruder had left him
with sore ribs and a bruised right cheek.

The ribs he could live with, but the wound
to his cheek was a problem as it was just the
kind of thing people would notice. While the
bruise might gain him sympathy, it would make
him look weak. And the last thing Matthew
wanted was to appear weak in front of Tessa.

From a bag on the passenger seat, he removed
the four containers of concealer makeup he'd
purchased that morning. Each was a slightly different shade. He experimented until he found the

one that best matched his skin tone, then covered the bruise.

Matthew studied his reflection again, touched up a spot where the bruise leaked through, and then deemed himself ready to go.

As he reached for his car door, his phone buzzed. He frowned, annoyed. He had a busy day ahead of him and didn't want to be bothered. But when he checked the screen and saw Stacy's name, he knew it was a call he couldn't ignore. Doing so now would raise too many questions.

"Hi," he answered.

"Matthew. Oh, my God. I just heard what happened last night. Are you okay?"

"You did? Oh, um, yeah. I'm okay. A little stiff today but fine."

"When you didn't show up for dinner, I thought you blew us off."

"I would never do that."

"I'm glad to hear it. Are you coming by the set today?"

"I want to, but I think I should probably rest. Would it be okay if I came tomorrow?"

"Of course. You're always welcome. The important thing is for you to take it easy right now. Do you need me to bring you anything?"

"That's kind of you to offer, but I'm good."

"If you change your mind, call me."

"I will."

He hung up and switched his phone to DO NOT DISTURB. No more interruptions.

From the passenger seat he grabbed his messenger bag, which contained all the items he would need, and made sure he had his stolen master keycard. Then he climbed out of his car and walked down to the hotel.

Three bored-looking fans stood near the driveway entrance, dangling signs by their sides proclaiming love for Tessa and Adriene, and even Mark Weldon. Matthew had no doubt they'd been waiting there for hours.

"Idiots," he muttered as he passed by them.

What a waste of time. The cast and crew were at the shoot today so there wouldn't be anyone for the trio of lookie-loos to get excited about until that evening at the earliest. Matthew could understand the enthusiasm, but scoffed at how little these fans clearly knew.

He headed into the hotel and proceeded directly to the elevators, walking with the confidence of someone who was a guest. As he stepped into the waiting area, one of the elevators opened and Ben Bacchetti exited.

Matthew froze.

What the hell was **he** doing here? He should have been at the set with everyone else.

Whereas Matthew was shocked, Ben didn't seem at all surprised and walked straight toward him, looking both concerned and happy to see him. "Matthew, how are you? How are you feeling?"

Matthew forced himself to smile. "Okay. Um, a bit sore, I guess."

"I'll bet."

When Ben's gaze paused on Matthew's face, Matthew subtly turned his head so that his bruised side was less visible.

"Here to see someone?" Ben asked.

Matthew's mind was still reeling with so much anger at coming face-to-face with Ben that it took him a moment to register the question. When he did, he inwardly cringed. He hadn't expected to run into anyone and hadn't prepared an answer as to why he was at the hotel. "No. I, um . . ."

His eyes caught sight of a sign on the wall, next to the elevators: MISSION SPA • THIRD FLOOR.

"I was going to the spa. They have a steam room. I thought it might help me feel better."

"That's a smart idea. A little steam should loosen you right up." Ben cocked his head, as if just thinking of something. "Listen, I need to get to the shoot soon but was going to grab a bite to eat first. If you'd be willing to put off the spa for a bit, I'd love for you to join me."

Matthew felt like gagging at the offer.

Having a meal alone with Ben Bacchetti had never been an item on Matthew's bucket list.

But just like with accepting Stacy's phone call, Matthew worried that if he said no, it might look suspicious. So he used every ounce of his willpower to keep smiling, and said, "I'd be honored. Thanks."

40

NENO ADDED THE AUDIO FILE TO THE NEW FOOTAGE of Rebecca and played the clip one more time. Everything looked and sounded as it should.

He glanced at his phone for what felt like the millionth time in the last hour and grimaced. Still no update from Kordo.

Had something happened? Had the person who'd been following Kordo caught up to him? Was he right now divulging where they were holding Rebecca Novak? Would he be so quick to fold?

Neno took a deep, steadying breath. No.

Kordo may have been apprehended, but he would never talk. Neno knew Kordo had been in worse situations and hadn't broken. A few

American moviemakers would never be as threatening as the butchers back home.

Neno had been hoping that after a few hours of hiding out, Kordo would have been able to shake whoever his tail was. His absence threw a wrench into the day's plan.

They were supposed to deliver that evening's video on another thumb drive. But that meant someone would need to take it to Vulin, and with Kordo unavailable, that was no longer possible. There was no way Neno would let Pavel do it. Pavel was the worst kind of stupid. The kind that thought he was smarter than everyone else.

Neno going himself was out of the question, too. He might not like Rebecca, but after Pavel's behavior with her earlier, and the multiple comments he made about her to Neno and Kordo, there was no way he was leaving him alone with her. It could turn out to be a disaster.

Which left sending the video via email once more as the only choice.

Janic would not be happy about the change if he found out. He had been the one who told them to leave thumb drives at various places throughout the Novaks' home.

"The more you can scare Novak, the greater his grief will be when his wife dies," Janic had said. "And I want him left shaking and destroyed. Do you understand?"

Neno had, and that was why he made the executive decision to leave his boss in the dark about the switch in plans. It was better this way.

He glanced at his phone again. Still nothing from Kordo.

Where is he?

With a frustrated grunt, Neno snatched up the phone and tapped out his colleague's number. He'd give him one more chance. If he didn't answer, maybe Neno **would** tell Janic about the change of plans and blame it on Kordo.

Better him than Neno.

TEDDY ALMOST DIDN'T HEAR THE RINGING OVER THE sound of the wind whipping by the Porsche. He shot a glance at the radio, wondering if he'd left the volume on low, but it was off.

When he heard a second ring, he realized it was coming from his jacket, which was lying on the passenger seat. His own phone was in a mount on the dash **and** on vibrate. The ringing had to be coming from the phone he'd taken from Kordo's car.

He retrieved the dead man's cell as it began ringing a third time. On the screen, the caller ID read: **NUMBER BLOCKED.**

Teddy's thumb hovered over the ACCEPT button for a second before he pulled away. Whoever was on the other end was likely one of Kordo's associates. Better if they remained unaware that someone else had their friend's phone, and, of course, that their friend was dead.

The mobile rang two more times before the screen went dark.

Teddy waited for the caller to try again, but the phone remained silent.

He stuck a wireless earbud into one ear and used his own phone to call Kevin.

The hacker answered with a yawned, "Morning."

"Check your clock. Where you are, it's already nighttime."

Teddy heard Kevin moving around on the other end.

"Huh. You're right."

"I usually am."

"So I've noticed."

"As much as I enjoy listening to you compliment me, there's something I'm hoping you can help me with."

"Color me surprised. What's up?"

"I have a phone I need unlocked."

"Since you're calling me on yours, I assume it belongs to someone else."

"Your grasp of logic continues to amaze me."

"All part of the services I provide. Do you know the number of the locked phone?"

"Unfortunately, no."

"Do you at least know where it is?"

"Sitting on the seat beside me."

"That I can work with. Is your Bluetooth on?"

"Yes."

"Give me a moment." After several seconds of silence, Kevin said, "I'm not in yet, but I'm connected to it. This might take a couple minutes."

"But you **can** get in, right?"

"Are you purposely trying to insult me?"

"Not this time."

"Stop talking and let me concentrate."

Over the next several minutes, the only signs that Kevin was still on the line was the occasional frustrated grunt.

Teddy soon reached the Santa Barbara city limits and then took the exit closest to the Novaks' estate.

After getting off the freeway, he'd only driven a few blocks away when Kevin said, "I'm in. Changing the screen lock code to 1-2-3-4. And . . . done."

"Can you do me a favor and check the call logs?"

"Why do you think I just changed the code? So you could do that yourself."

"I'm driving. I'd rather not be in another potential car accident today."

"Another?"

"Not important. Just check the logs."

"There are twenty-one incoming calls, all

listed as 'number blocked.' I assume you want me to check the outgoing, too?"

"If you didn't, I'd be disappointed."

"And we'd never want that." The line went quiet for a moment. "Wow. There's nothing there at all. The user either never initiated a call or he was diligent at erasing the log."

"Any way to find out what those blocked numbers are?"

Kevin clicked his tongue against the roof of his mouth several times. "It's possible, but might take some time."

"How much time?"

"Not sure. Could be a few hours. Could be a few days."

"We don't have a few days. We need to find the phone or phones those numbers belong to. And track them. There's a very good chance one of them is located where Rebecca Novak is being held."

"Oh. Got it. I'll get right on it. But if it's a cell phone, I may only be able to identify an area."

"That's better than what we have now. Let me know as soon as you have something."

41

LUNCH WITH BEN WAS AS SOUL-SUCKING AS
Matthew anticipated. Sitting there, across the table from the very man he hated more than anyone else in the world, was almost too much to bear.

Matthew deserved an Oscar for his performance. Hell, he deserved **all** the Oscars.

The small talk between him and Ben while they waited for their food to arrive had been so mind numbing, it was a small miracle he hadn't launched himself across the table and jammed his knife into Ben's chest.

"I hear you're in Santa Barbara on vacation," Ben said.

Matthew nodded.

"From L.A.?"

"Yep."

"Is that where your family's from?"

"No. Back east. Near Chicago." A lie, but as if he'd tell Ben the truth.

"I love Chicago. Any brothers and sisters?"

"Nope, just me."

And on and on the questions went, each forcing Matthew to create another falsehood.

The absolute worst was when Ben asked, "So tell me, Matthew, what is it you want to do with your life?"

Though he looked and sounded earnest, Matthew knew it was a ruse. People like Ben only cared about money and power. That was the sole reason he was with Tessa, Matthew knew. She brought Ben the prestige and respect he would never be able to obtain on his own.

Thankfully, the talk ebbed when their food arrived, and for several minutes Matthew was able to pretend he was eating by himself.

Of course, Ben didn't stay silent for long. "If I didn't tell you this already, I'm very impressed by what you did last night. Most people wouldn't have noticed the guy watching Billy, and even if they did, they wouldn't have done anything about it. Not you, though."

"It was nothing special," Matthew said.

"You're wrong. It was very special. You're a doer, Matthew. And I appreciate people like that." He reached into his pocket and pulled out a business card and a pen. He wrote something on the card and then held it out to Matthew. "I'd like you to have this."

Matthew took the card and immediately recognized the Centurion Studios logo on it. Printed below the logo was Ben's name, and beneath that the title PRESIDENT. There was also the studio's address and a phone number Matthew knew as belonging to Ben's office. At the very bottom was Ben's handwritten addition, a second phone number.

Ben pointed at it. "That's to my personal cell phone. If you need anything, don't hesitate to call me. And if you're ever interested in a job in the movies, let me know."

"Thank you. I will."

Matthew's smile was genuine this time. Not because he planned on asking Ben for a job, but because Ben had just provided the missing piece to Matthew's plan.

THE SUN WAS NEARING THE HORIZON BY THE TIME Matthew finished the task he'd come to the Santa Barbara Hills Hotel to do. He had hoped to have been long gone by now, but his encounter with Ben had ruined any chance of that happening.

Most of his time on the hotel's roof that

afternoon had been spent working out the best way to execute his plan. Once he had a direction he was happy with, he'd practiced it over and over, and then spent additional time coming up with several contingencies, in case he had to change tactics on the fly. While he couldn't completely remove the possibility of failure, he'd certainly reduced its chances.

Now that he had Ben's cell number, Matthew no longer had to worry about how he was going to trick Ben into coming up to the roof. His earlier plans all had revolved around risky invites that may not have worked, but now that he had direct access to his new "friend," when the time came, all he had to do was place a simple phone call enticing him up. Once Ben arrived at the rooftop door, Matthew would render him unconscious with the choke hold he'd learned from a how-to video online. Next, he'd inject Ben with the heroin Matthew had bought in L.A., and which was now hidden under a roof vent.

After giving the drug time to take effect, Matthew would rouse Ben enough to get him on his feet. At that point, it would be a simple matter of guiding Tessa's husband to the edge of the roof and giving him a nudge.

Matthew was confident the five-story fall would be more than enough to ensure Ben would no longer be an obstacle to Matthew and Tessa's future together.

He turned his back to the waning sun and looked across the roof. Everything was in place for the trap he would soon spring, including the pistol he'd hidden in case anything went awry.

For a moment, he considered putting his plan into motion tonight. The sooner Ben was dead, the sooner Tessa would be Matthew's, after all. But as tempting as that was, Matthew knew it would be better not to rush it.

Tomorrow would be soon enough. That would give him one final glorious day on set with Tessa before everything changed. And it would be thrilling to watch Ben hanging around the shoot, not knowing that his hours were numbered.

Matthew headed downstairs, grinning from ear to ear. By midnight tomorrow, Centurion Studios would need a new studio head.

42

"MR. BARNETT," THE NOVAKS' ACTING ESTATE
manager announced.

The woman, who had introduced herself as
Carina, moved out of the way so Teddy could
enter the Novaks' library.

Inside, Mori sat on one of the couches, a laptop
open on the coffee table, while over by the windows Carl Novak paced the length of the room.

Teddy checked his watch. It was a minute
after six p.m. "No video yet, I assume."

Mori glanced up. "Not yet."

"Is anyone checking elsewhere in the house in
case it's on a thumb drive again?"

Taking Vulin out of Janic's control had hopefully severed the kidnappers' access to the house,
and made it unlikely the video would arrive that

way. But there was always the chance the former estate manager hadn't been the only one who'd been coerced into doing Janic's bidding.

"Carina is. And before you ask, Carl trusts her."

"I don't mean to sound callous, but he trusted Vulin, too."

Novak paused mid-step and looked as if he was going to snap something in response. But then he continued walking without saying a word.

"True," Mori conceded, then stood and walked over to the liquor cabinet. He picked up a twenty-one-year-old bottle of Hibiki Suntory whisky. "Something to drink?"

"Thanks, but not right now," Teddy said.

Mori poured two glasses and carried one to Novak.

"I'm not thirsty," Novak said.

When he tried to walk by, Mori stepped in front of him. "This isn't for thirst. Take it."

"I'm fine."

"You're not."

Novak's lips pressed together in a thin line before he expelled an angry breath and took the glass. He downed the contents in a single gulp.

Mori held out his untouched drink. "Another?"

Novak looked momentarily unsure, then he exchanged the empty glass for the full one and drained it, too.

"Better?"

"Marginally."

"I'll take marginally." Mori turned to Teddy. "Do you have any update from your contact?"

"I talked to him on my way here. He has a strong lead he's following."

Novak stopped and whipped around. "He does? Does that mean he's close?"

"I would say closer than he was. Beyond that, I wouldn't want to speculate." Before Novak could ask another question, Teddy added, "Also, I think one of the kidnappers followed me this afternoon."

"What?"

Teddy would have preferred to keep his encounter with Kordo to himself for now, but he knew it was likely to make it onto local news websites, at the very least, and probably receive some airtime. Keeping it secret would be useless.

"He was spotted the last couple days near the set of the movie we're here to film. I was concerned enough to ask my contact to look into him. Turns out he worked for Zoran Janic."

"You said 'worked.' He doesn't work for him anymore?" Novak said.

"He doesn't work for anyone anymore."

Novak's brow furrowed in confusion. "What do you mean? Was he arrested?"

"I believe either he or one of his colleagues saw me the night Stone and I met with the both of you and became suspicious of my connection to you. My contact thinks he was waiting for me at the film set, but I spotted him first and began following him. He noticed, and in his attempt to get away, lost control of his vehicle. At the time, I was following him up the side of a mountain. The road was narrow and had a steep drop-off. He was going faster than he should. And . . ." Teddy paused. "He didn't survive."

"He's dead?" Novak stared at him, incredulous. "He could have told us where she was."

"Which is exactly what we were hoping to learn from him. And if I could have kept him from crashing, I would have. But telekinesis is not one of my talents."

"Did he have any information on him?" Mori asked. "Maybe something that might point your contact in the right direction?"

Teddy didn't want to tell them about Kordo's phone just yet. It was too loose of a thread, and he didn't want to get their hopes up. But before he could say something to deflect the question, the laptop on the coffee table emitted a soft bing.

All three of them swiveled toward the computer.

Mori reached the couch a moment before Teddy and Novak. Displayed on the screen was an email inbox. At the top of the box sat a new message, the subject line reading: **YOUR WIFE**.

Mori clicked on it.

The email contained only a video file and no text.

"Play it," Novak said.

Mori opened the file and started the video.

The now familiar setting of Rebecca's prison cell was visible on the screen, the only changes being the number on the wall and Rebecca's position on the cot. This time the number was two. As for Rebecca, she sat at the edge of her bed, her arms resting on her thighs, and stared directly into the camera, unblinking.

Novak ran a hand through his hair. "She looks even worse today."

Teddy wasn't so sure about that. Though he only knew her from the videos, there was something in her steady gaze that made him think the defiance he'd seen in the days prior was not only still there but had strengthened.

He cocked his head. For the first time, the audio was different. When it finished, he said, "Play it again."

Mori clicked the PLAY arrow again, and Teddy looked away from the screen to concentrate on the words.

"In two days at noon, you will be sent an account number. You will have two hours to transfer ten million dollars into it. At six p.m., if the money is received, you will be told where to find your wife. Our warning from before still stands. Do not contact the police or any other agency. Do not contact the press. If you do, you will never see your precious Rebecca alive again."

"They've been counting down until they want Carl to pay them?" Mori said. "Why not just have him do it immediately?"

"It's about control," Teddy said.

Novak nodded, more to himself than the others. "Janic wants me to suffer the same way he did before Leon died." He locked eyes with Teddy. "Maybe I should just wait and pay the ransom."

"Given who's behind it and the past you share, I'm sure the ransom is only smoke and mirrors."

"You surely can't mean . . ."

"They have no intention of returning Rebecca alive."

Novak grabbed the back of the couch for support, his eyes glazing over. "Forty-eight hours." He said this as if he couldn't grasp the meaning of the words. "Maybe . . . maybe we **should** call in the FBI."

"That's not a good idea."

"You can't expect me to sit here and do nothing."

"You aren't doing nothing. You have my contact looking for her. I guarantee you that he has a much better chance of finding her than the FBI would."

"How could you possibly know that?"

"What do you think the kidnappers will do if they find out you've gone to the FBI? And they **will** find out, because the FBI will bring in everyone they can. Including the SBPD. You're a big name, they're not going to handle this lightly. Your house will be flooded by law enforcement personnel, and there will be no missing that something is up."

Uncertainty crowded into Novak's eyes.

"I'm sorry, Carl, but your wife wasn't taken for money. This is revenge, pure and simple. Whether you pay the ransom or not, when that clock reaches zero, they will kill her. And if you involve the authorities, Janic's people won't wait the two days to do it."

Mori put a hand on Novak's shoulder. "He's right. We need to stay the course."

Novak looked on the verge of collapse as he said to Teddy, "Promise me your man can find her."

"I can't do that. But I can promise he will do everything in his power to make that happen, and that he's Rebecca's best chance."

"Can you at least tell him to please hurry?"

"That I can do."

43

TEDDY WANTED NOTHING MORE THAN TO GO straight up to his suite once he arrived back at the hotel. But after tossing his keys to the valet and striding toward the lobby, Matthew walked out of the building, right into Teddy's path.

The moment Matthew saw him he jammed to a stop. For half a second, he looked like a kid caught in the act of sneaking out of a house.

Then, just as quickly as it had appeared, the surprise vanished from his face, and a smile that didn't reach beyond his lips took its place. "Good evening, Mr. Barnett."

"Hello, Matthew. I didn't expect to see you here."

"I just stopped by to see Adriene and Stacy, but they're not around."

"I think they're scheduled to shoot for another hour."

"Oh. That explains it." Matthew laughed at himself. "I must have misheard her message. I thought she said they were getting off early."

Something was definitely up. Matthew was trying way too hard to act cool.

"This is the movie business. No one ever gets off early."

"I was going to see if she and Adriene were up for getting a drink tonight. I guess I'll come back later."

Matthew started to move around Teddy, but Teddy stepped in his way. "I haven't had the chance to thank you for what you did last night. I really appreciate it."

"It's okay. Really, I just happened to be in the right place at the right time, that's all."

"Don't sell yourself short. What you did was very brave."

Matthew smiled sheepishly. "I couldn't let him steal all your stuff."

"Thank you for that. I'm curious, how did you know to follow him?"

"Oh, well, I noticed him when I was waiting at the bar for Stacy, and realized he was one of the guards from the set. And then when you walked through the lobby on your way out, he fixated on you. It was strange. I thought he was going to follow you out, but instead he went to the elevators.

"It seemed fishy, you know. Gave me a bad feeling, so I followed him up to your suite." Matthew shrugged, then quickly added, "I mean, I didn't know it was your suite at the time. Tessa told me."

"How did you know he was in the room?"

"The door was propped open, and I could hear him opening drawers. I knocked. I was going to pretend I'd gone into the wrong room if it turned out I'd made a mistake about him."

"That was quick thinking on your part," Teddy said, hiding his skepticism from his voice. Matthew's version of events definitely did not match what Teddy had seen on the video. Matthew had most certainly not knocked.

"Yeah, but then he attacked me before I could even say hello."

Teddy could see the hint of a bruise on Matthew's face, peeking out from under a layer of makeup. Interesting. "How do you feel today?"

Matthew touched his side. "My ribs ache a bit, but I'll be okay."

Teddy smiled sympathetically. "Maybe next time you should think twice before doing something that'll get you beaten up. Not that I don't appreciate your efforts."

"I'll try to remember that."

Teddy patted him on the shoulder. "I need to make some phone calls, so I won't keep you any longer. But I owe you. I won't forget. Thanks again, Matthew. Have a good night."

"You, too." Matthew started to walk away, then hesitated and looked back. "Mr. Barnett?"

"Yes?"

"I might be wrong, but I thought I saw him walking by the pool a little while ago."

"The man who broke into my room?"

"Yeah. He was pretty far away, so I can't be sure. But it sure looked like him."

"What time was this?"

"Maybe half an hour ago? Around five-thirty?"

"Thank you, Matthew. I'll keep an eye out for him."

Teddy watched him walk away, knowing without a doubt now that Matthew was hiding something. Not only had Matthew been acting cagey throughout their conversation, but there's no way he had seen the ghost of Kordo at the pool.

It wasn't just the obvious lie. Teddy's well-honed senses were shouting that Matthew was trying to create a distraction. But from what, he had no idea.

Back in his suite, Teddy called Mike Freeman and told him what had gone on that day.

"I'm sure no one has ever told you your life is dull," Freeman said. "But there **is** something to be said about waking up in the morning and not worrying about potentially dying before the end of the day."

"I never worry about that. Either it happens or it doesn't. And so far, still alive."

"There's always a first time."

"You mean last."

"You say tomato . . . Do you think Rebecca's kidnappers will send someone else after you?"

"I think there's a decent chance. Which is why I need your men on set to keep an eye out for anyone suspicious. If they spot someone, let me know. Whatever we do, we need to be sure to take him alive this time."

"I'll let Rivera know."

"Thanks. One more thing. I'd like you to do a background check on Matthew Wagner. In addition to his part in the shooting the other day, he's also the guy who stopped the intruder in my room."

"Is he now? That's quite a coincidence."

"It could be just that, but there's something not right about him."

"I'll get some people on it."

After hanging up, Teddy headed into the bathroom to wash off the dust and dry sweat that still clung to him from his descent to Kordo's car.

He was halfway undressed when his phone buzzed. He checked the screen and hit the speaker button. "You're up early."

"More like I haven't gone to sleep yet," Vesna said. It was barely four a.m. in Croatia. "We know where Janic is keeping Vulin's family."

"They're still alive?"

"As best we can tell, yes."

"Do you think you can free them?"

"Teddy, my friend. It sounds like you are doubting me."

"My apologies. I forgot for a moment who I was talking to."

"That's better."

44

THIRTY MINUTES AFTER HANGING UP WITH TEDDY, part one of Vesna Martic's two-part plan to rescue Andrew Vulin's family commenced.

The first stop was at a warehouse belonging to Simon Lazovic. Lazovic had been trying to elbow his way into Janic's business for years, swiftly becoming one of Janic's biggest rivals, making him the perfect patsy for Vesna's plan.

Six months earlier, Lazovic's people had stolen a weapons shipment off a train in nearby Serbia. Though the crime was officially unsolved, everyone knew who was responsible. Which meant if the pilfered weapons were used—for instance—in an attack on an enemy's stronghold where a family of innocent civilians just happened to be detained, blame would fall at Lazovic's doorstep. If Vesna was really lucky, it might even start a war between the rival organizations.

Vesna had learned from a contact that the weapons were being held at this particular warehouse, and that the building was guarded by half a dozen men. Two guards walked the perimeter, while the rest were stationed inside, on the ground floor.

After observing the pair outside for twenty minutes, Vesna noted two things. The first was that the guards patrolled in a pattern that left a four-minute gap in coverage at the warehouse's back corner. Second, near that corner on the third floor was a broken window. Though most of the glass was still intact, there was a section missing that looked large enough to reach through.

When the guards disappeared from sight again, she and the three men she'd brought with her used several pipes that ran up the side of the building to climb to the window. Vesna stuck her hand through the break and found the window's latch. The window swung open a bit nosier than she would have liked, so as soon as she and her men scrambled inside, they pressed against the wall, waiting for someone to show up.

When no one did, they found a stairwell and headed down. The room they wanted was in the basement, which meant passing the ground floor where Lazovic's other men were.

After signaling her colleagues to wait, Vesna

eased down the final flight of stairs to the first-floor landing. She listened at the door, then slipped a microcamera through the space at the bottom. The wireless camera was attached to a rod that she used to move it.

She watched the feed on her phone and saw that the corridor outside ran parallel to the door. She aimed the camera left, spotted no one, and then swung the lens to the right. One guard sat in a chair, next to a door that was approximately twenty meters away. His head moved slightly back and forth, like he was nodding to someone who was talking to him. But he was the only one in the hall.

She zoomed the lens in on him. He was wearing earbuds, connected to a phone in his lap. Perhaps he was on a call, or maybe watching a video. Either way, he was distracted.

She motioned to her men, and once they joined her, they all continued down to the basement.

The weapon's storage room was exactly where Vesna had been told it would be. Even the three sets of dead bolts were as advertised. All were high-end security models that would have given a normal thief a massive headache. But Vesna was no normal thief and was more than familiar with how to finesse the tumblers into place. Within seventy-five seconds, all three locks were undone.

The room beyond was stocked with all manner of deadly hardware and ammunition. Some weapons looked as if they'd come straight from the manufacturers, while others appeared old enough to have been used in the Bosnian war a few decades earlier.

As they had discussed ahead of time, Gregor laid out the duffel bags he'd been carrying, while Vesna, Josef, and Emmanuel began collecting weapons that were from the train robbery.

Handguns went into one duffel, rifles into another, and ammunition into the smaller third bag. One and a half minutes after entering the room, they were back in the corridor, each of Vesna's men carrying one of the bags.

Vesna relocked the dead bolts, and they headed out the way they'd come, Lazovic's people having no idea they were ever there.

Twenty-three minutes later and fifteen miles to the northeast, Vesna's team was joined by four others, a block from Janic's hideout, where the hostages were being held.

The team was made up entirely of former undercover operatives from intelligence agencies of various European countries. Some had once been enemies, but time had a way of shifting alliances.

Vesna and Gregor handed out the weapons. As instructed, no one had brought their own.

"Rules of engagement?" asked a man who had once worked for the Bulgarians.

"The only ones who walk out of there alive are the hostages and us."

A Greek woman who had spent most of her working life in the Middle East grinned. "Sounds like fun."

Vesna described the layout of the building and explained her plan. When she finished, she asked for any questions. There were none.

"In and out before the sun comes up," she said. On the eastern horizon sat the barest hint of the coming day.

"Are you taking us out to breakfast after?"

"Of course. I'm not a barbarian."

Breaching the three-story hideout was even simpler than the warehouse. Years of use by Janic's organization had left the guards who worked there complacent. While the main entrances and exits were secured, the roof could be easily reached by placing a ladder over to it from the adjacent building.

The door to the roof stairwell was locked by a chain and padlock wrapped around the bars on the inside. Unfortunately for Janic's people, whoever had secured the door had left enough slack in the chain that the door could be opened several inches, allowing one of Vesna's people to slip through the jaws of a bolt cutter. A couple of snips and the chain was broken.

Several rooms on the top floor were filled with bunk beds. While most were empty, four were in use. Vesna's team delivered the men sleeping in them to a more permanent slumber before heading downstairs.

They checked the second floor, but the rooms there were empty.

When they reached the first, they heard muffled voices coming from beyond the stairwell door. Vesna knelt in front of it and deployed her microcamera again. She could see light spilling out of several rooms in the hallway on the other side.

She signaled for four of her team to deal with the rooms on the left, while she and the others would deal with those on the right. She then pointed at the door hinges and nodded her chin at Emmanuel. After he removed a can of lubricant from his pack and drizzled oil onto the hinges, Vesna eased open the door.

Most of the voices they heard were coming from the direction she and her group were headed.

Inside the first room, two men sat in front of a TV—one watching, the other asleep.

Vesna and a German operative quietly approached the targets from behind. Once they were both in position, Vesna gave the signal.

The German looped his arm around the sleeping man's neck and cut off his air. Vesna's target was awake and more likely to yell, so she dealt with him swiftly by placing her silencer against his temple and pulling the trigger.

The most difficult of the remaining rooms was the one in which Janic's people ate their meals. Five people were inside. Three sat at the only table, one stood in front of a refrigerator, and the last stared at a humming microwave oven.

Vesna assigned each of her colleagues a different man at the table and reserved the two who were standing for herself.

They rushed inside and pulled their triggers. As soon as Vesna's first shot was off, she adjusted her aim to her second target and fired again.

All of Janic's men collapsed, either onto the table or the floor. Given the professional level of those she had recruited, it wasn't surprising that none of the targets required a second bullet. The other half of Vesna's team had encountered only four men and had dealt with them in the same efficient manner.

Within ten minutes of stepping into the Janic hideout, the building was secured.

The problem was they hadn't found any sign of the hostages yet.

"Check again," Vesna ordered. "Every room. They must be here somewhere."

It was Vesna herself who discovered the hidden door in the back of a first-floor storeroom. The narrow space beyond it was barely big enough for the four scared-looking people crammed inside.

◆ ◆ ◆

AT NINE-THIRTY P.M., TEDDY RECEIVED A VIDEO CALL from Vesna. In Croatia, it was half past six the following morning.

From the way the picture bounced around, he guessed she was in a vehicle.

"I have news," she said and turned her camera so that it pointed into the back of a panel van, where several people sat against the walls. From the size and calm demeanor of the group on one side, Teddy knew they had to be the members of Vesna's team. As for the four tired- and dazed-looking ones on the other side—

"Vulin's family?"

Vesna aimed the camera back at herself. "As promised."

"Anyone hurt?"

"Some bruises. A few cuts. One has a broken arm. I also don't think they've been given much to eat. But with a little rest, a few meals, and some medical attention, they should be fine."

"What about Janic's men? Any problems?"

"Why do you continue to underestimate me?"

"Because I'm a damn fool?"

"Finally, you are talking sense."

"Humor me anyway."

She rolled her eyes. "Of course, there were no problems. They were all very cooperative, and none of them will be bothering anyone ever again."

"And Janic won't be able to trace what happened back to you, right?"

"Okay, now you're seriously insulting me."

"It's called a debrief. You remember what those are, don't you?"

"Fine. No, he won't be able to trace it back to me. Or you, if that's your real concern. We left just enough clues to point him in the direction of a rival."

"That sounds like the perfect solution. And just for the record, I never doubted you."

"Perhaps you should have led with that."

"But winding you up is so much fun."

Her eyes narrowed, but she said nothing.

"Where are you taking Vulin's family?" he asked.

"Someplace Janic will never find them."

"Thank you, Vesna. I owe you."

"Yes. You do."

45

LIKE MOST MORNINGS, JANIC STARTED HIS DAY WITH a swim in his villa's indoor pool. He was on his twenty-third lap when he heard something slapping the water.

He stopped mid-stroke and looked toward the noise. Orin, one of his lieutenants, knelt at the edge of the pool and waved a hand.

Whatever he needed to tell Janic could not be good. Janic's men knew never to disturb him when he was swimming, unless it was an extreme emergency.

He swam to the end and scowled. "What is it?"

"We have a situation."

"What kind of situation?"

Orin's expression was normally one of stony

indifference, but now his eyes shifted uncomfortably and his mouth twitched, as if not wanting to say anything else.

"What kind of situation?" Janic repeated, spitting out each syllable like a gunshot.

"It's our place on Salata Road. Someone raided it."

Janic stared at him, sure that he'd misheard. "Salata?"

"Yes, sir."

That was the building in which Andrew Vulin's family was being held. "I assume you are here to tell me it was unsuccessful and whoever tried getting in is either dead or captured."

Orin swallow hard. "No, sir. Our people were all . . . killed."

It took Janic a second before he could speak. "Everyone?"

Orin gulped again. "Yes."

"The hostages. What happened to them?"

"They . . . they appear to have escaped in the chaos."

"They **what**?"

"There's no sign of them."

Janic grabbed the lip of the pool and pulled himself out so fast Orin had to jump back to get out of the way.

"Towel," Janic growled.

Orin hurried to the chair where a folded towel lay, grabbed it, and brought it to his boss.

Janic dried off as he walked briskly toward the exit. "Who was in charge there?"

"Marceta."

"And he's dead, too?"

"Yes, sir."

Janic cursed. Marceta had been a rising talent in Janic's organization. Young, but levelheaded and smart. "How many assholes did our people take out?"

"As far as we can tell, none."

Janic halted and stared at Orin. "None?"

"No, sir. It appears that, um, Marceta and his team were caught by surprise."

"What do you mean surprise? They didn't even get a shot off?"

"That's what it looks like."

"How is that even possible?"

"We're not entirely sure. We're still investigating."

"Do we at least know who it was?"

Once again, Orin hesitated.

Janic narrowed his eyes. "What are you not telling me?"

"There are indications that Simon Lazovic's people might be involved."

"What indications?"

"A pistol was found. Not one of ours. Its serial number matches a gun from that shipment Lazovic stole last year. From that train heist in Serbia."

The pressure in Janic's skull increased tenfold.
Simon Lazovic.

That son of a bitch had been nothing but trouble. It was a little strange that he had targeted this particular hideout, but one-off attacks like this between groups wasn't uncommon. Janic needed to put an end to him. But that would need to wait. Right now, he had something more important and urgent that needed his full attention.

In less than two days, his revenge on Carl Novak would be completed. Until the man received the devastating news of his wife's death, Janic didn't want to focus on anything else.

After that, he could worry about Lazovic.

"Find out everything you can," he said. "We need to be certain it's them before we do anything."

"Yes, sir."

46

"YOU'RE MARK WELDON!" A BEAUTIFUL, DARK-HAIRED woman stood in the middle of the Santa Barbara Hills Hotel lobby, one hand gripping the suitcase she'd been pulling, the other pointing at Teddy, as if she needed to make sure he knew she was talking about him.

"Would you believe me if I told you I wasn't?"

"It **is** you. I'd recognize your voice anywhere." She let go of her suitcase and fumbled with her purse. "Can I get a picture?"

Teddy could see Stone waiting for him at the entrance to the restaurant for breakfast. But as Ben often reminded him, it never hurt to give a fan a few moments. "Sure."

After the woman found her phone, she hurried to him and pressed her shoulder against his.

From over at the check-in desk, Teddy noticed one of the hotel security officers moving toward them. The staff there had done a great job at keeping fans from bothering the **Storm's Eye** cast so far. No doubt the officer's intention was to do the same for Mark Weldon now.

Teddy caught the guard's eye and shook his head, letting her know it was okay. With a nod, she returned to her post next to the desk.

The fan's hand shook as she raised her phone to take a selfie with him.

"Why don't I do it?" Teddy took the phone from her.

"Thank you. I'm sorry. I'm just so nervous."

Teddy held it in front of them. "Smile." He took several shots and returned the phone.

As the woman scrolled through the images, Teddy asked, "Did I do all right?"

She beamed. "These are great. My sister is going to flip out. Thank you so much."

"You're very welcome."

He left her looking at her screen and headed over to the restaurant, where Stone was shaking his head, a sly smile on his face.

"I don't think I'll ever get used to watching that kind of thing happen to you."

"Why, Stone, are you jealous?"

"Of you getting stopped in hotel lobbies by beautiful women? Absolutely."

Once they were seated and their orders taken,

Teddy brought Stone up to speed on his search for Rebecca.

"I know I don't have to remind you that you're running out of time," Stone said.

"Correct me if I'm wrong, but isn't that what you just did?"

"Don't you know you're never supposed to call a lawyer on his tricks?"

"And who would have made that rule? A lawyer?"

"Who else?"

Across the room, Ben entered the restaurant, and Stone waved for him to join them.

After Ben placed his breakfast order, he said to Teddy, "No more unwanted visitors?"

"None that I'm aware of."

"Glad to hear it. I treated Matthew to lunch yesterday, and talked to him again about what happened. I have to say, he's lucky he wasn't hurt worse."

"You had lunch with Matthew? Where? What time?"

"Right here, in this restaurant." Ben thought for a moment. "Around one, I think."

"Was it a planned thing?"

Ben shook his head. "We bumped into each other in the lobby. Why?"

"Just curious. I thought he would have spent the day in bed, after what he went through."

"He said he was here to use the spa. Thought it would help him feel better."

"I hope it did."

When Teddy had run into Matthew last evening, Matthew had given Teddy the impression he'd only been at the hotel for a short time. If he'd spent the afternoon at the hotel spa, why hadn't he said so?

Something wasn't adding up.

But there was a way Teddy could find the answers. He would just have to wait a bit before he could check.

PETER LEANED OUT FROM HIS MONITOR. "ONE more time."

Teddy and Logan returned to their starting positions, out of the camera frame.

"Action," Peter called.

Teddy sprinted to the parked car and yanked the door open. As he climbed in, Logan raced into the shot.

"Storm! Where the hell do you think you're going?"

"I'll be back. I promise. But there's something I need to do first."

Logan brandished a gun. "The only thing you need to do right now is get out of that car."

Teddy started the vehicle. "If you're going to shoot me, then shoot me. Otherwise, get out of my way." He shifted the car into reverse and looked behind him.

"Cut!" Peter shouted. "Perfect. Excellent work, gentlemen."

Normally, Teddy would watch a replay of the scene, but between his unanswered questions about Matthew and the clock clicking down on Rebecca's life, he had no time to spare.

He gave Peter a wave and headed to Mark Weldon's trailer.

Before being called to the set earlier, he'd begun searching through hotel security footage from the previous day, looking for signs of Matthew. Before it was time to film his scene, he'd only had time to establish Matthew's lunchtime arrival and how he subsequently ran into Ben in the lobby.

Now back at his laptop, he picked up the search where he'd left off. The first thing he confirmed was that after Matthew left the restaurant, he had remained at the hotel. He did not go to the spa, however.

Switching between camera feeds, Teddy followed Matthew, after he parted with Ben, through the building and into a side corridor, where he stopped in front of a door marked STAIRS. Matthew looked both ways, clearly checking that he was alone, and then entered the stairwell.

It took Teddy a minute to locate the feeds

of the cameras covering the stairwell and pick up Matthew's trail again. To Teddy's surprise, Matthew went all the way up to the roof exit, which had a sign on it that read EMPLOYEES ONLY.

Matthew removed something from his pocket and waved it over the pad next to the door. When he pushed the door handle, the door opened, and he stepped outside.

"Huh," Teddy said.

Matthew apparently had a keycard. Which was odd, given that Teddy was sure he wasn't staying at the hotel. And even if he was, Teddy was willing to bet every cent he'd ever made working in Hollywood that the keycards hotel guests received wouldn't open that door.

How did Matthew end up with a keycard that granted him access to places only authorized employees could go?

Teddy thought about the video of Matthew hunched in front of the entrance to Billy's suite. Matthew had said the door had been ajar, but his actions hadn't matched the description. His actions **did** match that of someone with a master keycard, however. And if that were the case, Matthew must have known the suite hadn't belonged to Kordo but was, in fact, Billy Barnett's.

Which begged yet another question: How would he know that?

Teddy tried to find any cameras on the roof,

but there were none. So, he did the next best thing and sped through the footage that covered the roof doorway, searching for the moment Matthew reappeared. He was beginning to think Matthew must have used a different way down, when Matthew finally reentered the stairwell.

Teddy checked the time stamp. He had left the roof approximately five minutes before Teddy had run into him in front of the hotel last evening. Meaning he'd been on the roof for approximately three hours.

Matthew had lied to Ben about going to the spa. And he'd lied to Teddy about being at the hotel for the short time he'd claimed; he'd been there for hours.

What could he have been doing up there for so long?

This was beginning to feel more insidious than just a white lie or two. Teddy needed answers, none of which he could find sitting in Mark Weldon's trailer.

Using his makeup kit, he turned himself back into Billy Barnett, then from the bag he'd brought with him that morning donned clothes more suitable to the film producer.

After checking himself in the mirror, he retrieved his phone and called Daniel Rivera, the new head of security at the shoot.

"How can I help you, Mr. Barnett?"

"Is Matthew Wagner on set today?" Though Teddy had seen Matthew earlier, that had been as Mark, not Billy.

"Yes, sir. He's sitting with Logan and Tessa."

"Do me a favor. If he leaves, call me."

"Is there something I should be concerned about?"

"Maybe. I'll let you know."

"Consider it done."

Teddy slipped his phone into his pocket and moved to the back door of his trailer. As the film's star, Mark was given one of the largest trailers. The only others with ones of similar size were Tessa, Peter, and Billy.

As Billy, Teddy had sent instructions for his and Mark's trailers to be positioned behind Tessa's and Peter's trailers and the other smaller units used by the rest of the cast. This effectively blocked both trailers from the view of most of the cast and crew. However, it did not guarantee there would be no one walking through the area at any given time.

When Teddy peeked through the window, he spotted a production assistant hurrying down the walkway just outside, clutching a cardboard box. After he disappeared, Teddy cracked the door open. He heard no footsteps nearby. The only noise was coming from the set.

He slipped out and left the location through a side barrier, manned by a single guard.

"Have a good day, Mr. Barnett," the guard said.

Teddy raised a finger to his lips, and with a mischievous smile said, "Shhh. If anyone asks, you didn't see me."

The guard grinned back. "You're the boss, sir. What you say goes."

"You have a bright future ahead of you."

Teddy returned to the hotel in one of the production vehicles. He hadn't planned on going back, but his need to figure out this Matthew situation had changed things.

He located the stairwell Matthew had taken and climbed it to the roof entrance.

He held his suite keycard over the pad next to the door. As he'd expected, the door remained locked.

He took a quick trip down to his suite and retrieved one of the items he'd picked up from his house—a black box about the size of a typical cell phone.

When he reached the roof door again, he flipped a switch on the side of the box and held the device over the pad. For five seconds, nothing happened. Then a tiny green light at the top of the pad lit up, and the door latch clicked.

Teddy pushed the door open and stepped onto the roof. The flat expanse was dotted with air vents, heating and cooling units, and groups of solar panels.

He searched for any signs of what Matthew

had been up to and, after several minutes, discovered a small bag tucked into a narrow space under one of the HVAC systems. Inside were two syringes and an unmarked bottle with what he assumed was some kind of drug.

Had Matthew come up here to get high?

He had seemed nervous when Teddy had run into him, but not out of control. Teddy would have noticed if Matthew's eyes had been dilated or red. And he hadn't picked up any other signs that Matthew had been on anything.

Perhaps he was good at hiding it.

Teddy continued looking around and discovered another package not far away. While the leather zip-top bag was identical to the one holding the syringes, instead of containing drugs, this one held a pistol.

Short of checking for fingerprints, Teddy had no way of knowing for sure if Matthew was connected to either bag. But only a fool at this point would not believe Matthew had put them there. And Teddy was no fool.

He pulled out his phone and called Mike Freeman.

"Where are we with the background check on Matthew Wagner?"

"Still waiting for confirmation on a few details, but . . ."

"But what?"

"Hold on a second." The line went silent for a

few moments. "Check your email. I've sent you what we have so far. You're not going to like it."

"Give me the highlights."

"Lowlights, more like it. So far, we've determined that he has at least seven aliases, and it won't surprise me if the final number is double that."

"You're right, I don't like it."

"That's just the start. Matthew has a lengthy arrest record."

"For what?"

"Stalking, harassment, breaking and entering, shoplifting. Only one conviction, though, but that occurred when he was a minor, so the record is sealed. There may be a way of finding out, if you want me to pursue it."

"Let's put a pin in that for now." The reason for his conviction wasn't as important as the fact he clearly had been living as if laws didn't apply to him. "What else have you learned? Any family? Friends?"

"He appears to have broken off contact with his family when he was released from juvenile detention at eighteen. We have found no indication of any friends."

"A loner."

"That would be my preliminary assessment, yes. Do you want me to have Rivera remove him from the set?"

"Not yet. Better to keep him where we can

watch him." Teddy opened the email and skimmed through the report. "I see he currently lives in Los Angeles. His address looks—"

"Like it's close to Centurion Studios? You're right. It's only four blocks away."

Teddy grimaced. "I don't see anything here about where he's staying in Santa Barbara."

"That's one of the things my people are still checking. Give me a moment." The line went quiet again. When Freeman returned, he said, "It looks like he's renting an Airbnb, about a mile from your hotel. I'll send you the address. We're waiting for final confirmation, but we have high confidence the information is correct."

"Do you have someone at your L.A. office who can check out his apartment?"

"Of course."

"Great. Do it. When do you think you'll have confirmation on the Airbnb?"

"Within thirty minutes."

Teddy's phone beeped with another call. He checked his screen and saw that it was Kevin.

"Let me know when you get that, and I'll check it out myself. I've got to run."

He clicked over to Kevin's call.

"Tell me you have good news."

"I figured out what number kept calling the locked cell phone, will that do?"

"Number? As in only one?"

"Yep. All the blocked number calls were from the same phone."

"I'd call that great news."

"I can't tell you precisely where it's located, but I've narrowed it down to six square blocks."

"That's better than the whole city. Kevin, you are my new favorite person."

"I wasn't before?"

47

AS MUCH AS TEDDY WANTED TO GO STRAIGHT TO
Matthew's Airbnb, finding Rebecca was the
priority. If Kevin's info on the phone's location
helped to find her, then that had to come first.

The six square blocks where Kordo's mysterious caller was likely located turned out to be
part of a business zone. Not the kind of area with
shops and restaurants, however, but one filled
with workshops and warehouses and other businesses that needed significant amounts of space.
Some of the properties were clearly in use while
others looked unoccupied.

Teddy fought the desire to drive down every
street and examine each building. Given Kordo's
interest in him, doing so would be a mistake.

The kidnappers clearly knew who he was, and he couldn't risk that he might be spotted.

So he remained on the periphery and examined as many of the places within the area as he could, through his binoculars.

Unfortunately, this did nothing to narrow things down. Rebecca could have been almost anywhere within the zone Kevin had identified. It was also possible she wasn't anywhere near here at all, and the phone calls had only been made from this area. It could all have been a decoy to hide where she really was.

As Teddy thought through the case, he began to form an idea, some way to zero in on the search area.

He called Kevin again. "I have a feeling I'm about to ask you to do the impossible."

"If you were trying to get my attention, you've done it."

"Had I known it was that easy, I would have used that line before. Here's what I'm wondering, can you track all the outbound internet activity from the area the calls came from?"

"Um, technically. What exactly are you looking for?"

"If everything stays to pattern, the kidnappers will send an email with another video of Rebecca tonight at 6:07 p.m. If any messages go out at that exact time from that area, there's a very good chance one will be the video. My question is, if that happens, can you then trace the email back to its source?"

"The answer is yes, but . . ."

"But what?"

"But there could be a lot of data to go through to find it. And if they're using any kind of encryption on their end, that would slow the process even more. But I have a better idea. Faster."

"Faster is good."

"It would mean you giving me access to your phone."

"I'm not sure we're at that point in our relationship yet."

"What? No, I promise I won't look at—"

"What's your idea?"

"We already know the other emails were sent from a cell phone. What do you think the chances are it's the same one that called the locked phone?"

"High."

"Okay, then. I should be able to modify your phone's location app so that the next time the other phone is turned on, you'll be alerted to where it is. If that happens at 6:07 p.m., it'll pretty much guarantee it's them. And you won't have to wait for me to hunt through the data."

"Are you sure that will work?"

"I was already testing the code before you called. And I can confidently say that it should probably work."

"Probably?"

"Almost certainly could work?"

"Not making me feel any better there, Kevin."

"How about this? I do the mod to your phone, and I also track the data like you suggested."

"That's a plan I can get behind. Feel free to have your way with my phone."

"That sounds—"

"Just do it."

After Kevin made the tweaks to Teddy's phone, Teddy checked the location app. The other phone showed as offline, location unknown.

While they'd been talking, a message had come in from Freeman, confirming Matthew's Santa Barbara Airbnb rental.

There was still an hour and a half until Teddy expected the video to be sent and, theoretically, the phone turning on. That would leave him with more than enough time to pay Matthew's temporary residence a visit.

Teddy found the rental in a quiet neighborhood, a few blocks from the beach. It was a studio apartment over a garage, next to the house where the owners lived.

A car was parked in the driveway. Not the Honda Accord Matthew had been seen driving, so it probably belonged to one of the people living in the house.

Donning the persona of a friend coming to visit Matthew, Teddy walked past the parked car to the stairs running up the outside of the garage. At the top, he paused at the apartment door and listened in case anyone was coming from the house to see who he was. When he was sure he'd been unobserved, he placed his ear against the door.

Silence.

He donned a pair of gloves and used his lock picks to let himself inside.

If not for the suitcase sitting near the bed, the place looked as if it were already waiting for its next tenant. Empty counters, chairs tucked under the small dining table, a bed made to what looked like military standard.

He finally saw signs of occupancy when he checked the bathroom. Laid out side by side on the counter were a toothbrush, a tube of toothpaste, a razor, and a can of shaving cream, the bottoms of each perfectly aligned. Piled on the floor at the other end of the room were a T-shirt and a pair of jeans. They seemed oddly out of place, given the neatness of everything else.

Teddy lifted the shirt with the toe of his shoe. Both it and the pants were covered in dirt.

What could Matthew have been doing that would have made such a mess?

Teddy moved back into the main room to conduct a more thorough search. In the kitchen trash can, he found more than a dozen fan magazines.

He removed a few and flipped through them.

In each, images had been cut out. All were from articles about Tessa.

He then laid Matthew's suitcase on its side and opened it. The only things it contained were several pieces of perfectly folded clothes. He closed the suitcase and returned it to where it was, then checked the nightstands and the dresser, both of which were empty.

As he started to turn away from the dresser, something caught his eye. A piece of thin, white cardboard appeared to be nestled between the back of the dresser and the wall.

He leaned in for a closer look.

It wasn't cardboard from a box, but rather thick poster board. He eased the dresser away from the wall just enough so that he could grab the top of the board and pull it up without it catching on anything.

Taped to it were all the pictures that had been cut out of the magazines. Most were of Tessa alone. But a few also featured Ben. At least, Teddy was pretty sure it was Ben. In each, Ben's face was scribbled over with a pen until it was completely covered.

Teddy's phone vibrated. When he pulled it out, he saw that Mike Freeman was video-calling him. That was unusual.

Teddy tapped ACCEPT and Freeman appeared on his screen.

Before Teddy could say hello, Freeman jumped

in. "My agent is inside Wagner's apartment in L.A. You need to see what she found."

"Don't tell me. Pictures of Tessa taped to the wall."

"How did you—"

Teddy turned the camera to the poster.

"Oh."

"Show me the space."

Freeman conferenced in his person in L.A. and introduced her as Karlena Driscoll. "Please show Mr. Barnett what you found."

With a nod, Driscoll flipped the camera. She was in a bedroom that had a bed in a corner, a desk against a wall, and no other furniture.

All four walls were covered in photo clippings.

"These three walls are dedicated to Miss Tweed," Driscoll said. She panned the camera over walls filled top to bottom with pictures of Tessa. Like with the board Teddy had found, in any picture in which Ben appeared with her, his face had been blacked out.

"And the last wall?" Teddy asked.

The camera switched to it. The images there were of people associated with Centurion Studios. Beneath every photo was a neat, handwritten label, identifying the person or persons in the shot. Teddy was featured twice, once as Billy Barnett and once as Mark Weldon.

As he'd started to suspect, Matthew's appearance at the film shoot was no accident.

The gunshots Matthew had "saved" Stacy and Adriene from likely had been his own doing, as a way of getting on set.

A way of getting close to Tessa.

"What do you want to do?" Freeman asked.

What Teddy wanted to do was to handle Rebecca's rescue and then the threat from Matthew separately. But no matter which way he looked at it, that was no longer an option. His ability to save Rebecca or not would be coming to a head within the hour. But there was also no way he would risk leaving Matthew anywhere near his friends. He would have to deal with them both.

Two birds, one stone.

Or, in this case, one Teddy.

"Call Rivera," Teddy told Freeman. "Make sure he doesn't let Matthew out of his sight. I'm heading to the set now."

Once Teddy was on the road again, he called Stacy. "How's the shoot going?"

"We're about a half hour behind schedule. Peter didn't like one of the shots, so they had to change the setup."

"So a normal day, then."

"Pretty much."

"Say, is Matthew Wagner there today?"

"He is. Why?"

"I'd like to take him out for dinner to thank him for what he did the other day."

"Aren't you Mr. Nice Guy."

"Just because I'm a movie producer doesn't mean I can't do something selfless, now and then."

"I don't know about that. Should I check Producers Guild guidelines to be sure, first?"

"How about we assume I'm right. Do me a favor, and let Matthew know I'll pick him up by the makeup trailers in about fifteen minutes. Oh, and make sure to mention to him that Tessa and Ben will be joining us." Matthew might beg out of dinner with only Billy, but Teddy was certain there was no way he'd miss a chance to eat with Tessa.

"Wow. Can I come, too?"

"Maybe next time."

"I'm holding you to that."

48

"QUIET ON THE SET."

Logan Chase put a hand next to his mouth and stage-whispered to Matthew, "I'll tell you the rest after."

Matthew smiled and nodded as if eager to hear more of Logan's story. In truth, the assistant director's announcement had come none too soon as far as Matthew was concerned. If he had to listen to one more minute of Logan humblebragging about how large a role he'd had in his first film, Matthew might strangle him on the spot.

Over at the camera, Peter gave Tessa and Adriene a few last-minute instructions. When he retreated to his monitor, the assistant director raised his electronic megaphone again and said, "Places, everyone."

Matthew's eyes were glued to Tessa. He loved watching her in the moments before she performed. Loved the way a calmness descended over her. Loved the moment when she would shut her eyes as Tessa Tweed and then open them as Vivica Storm.

Had there ever been a greater actress in the history of film? For Matthew, the answer was an emphatic no.

Peter eyed the set, then shouted, "Action!"

Tessa and Adriene hurried into the frame. They looked anxious and scared, exactly the way people would if worried about the well-being of someone important to them.

The scene had no dialogue. It consisted only of Tessa and Adriene entering the shot and walking quickly away from the camera.

Matthew knew from the script he'd procured that the scene would be part of a montage near the end of the film. The nieces were on what would be a failed quest to save their uncle's life. But while they would be unsuccessful, it would be Tyler Storm's sacrifice that would save them from paying the price for his past.

When the two actors turned the corner at the end of the block, Peter yelled, "Cut. Let's do it again."

"Reset, everyone," the AD announced.

Naturally, much to Matthew's annoyance, Logan took advantage of the pause between takes to restart his story. "As you can imagine, I was worried they were going to kick me off when the—"

"Matthew?"

Matthew turned to see Stacy walking up. He smiled, more in relief than anything else.

"Hey, Stacy. I was wondering where you'd gone off to."

She glanced past him at Logan. In a low voice that only he could hear, she whispered, "We've left you all alone with him, haven't we? Sorry about that."

"It's fine," he whispered back. "But I think I know more about his life now than I do my own."

Logan leaned toward them. "Are you two talking about me?"

"Not every conversation is about you," Stacy ribbed him.

The actor smirked. "I refuse to believe that." One of the things that kept people from truly disliking Logan was his ability to poke fun at himself.

To Matthew, Stacy said, "I was wondering if you have plans this evening."

Matthew almost laughed. Boy, did he ever. Tonight was the night he would rid the world of Ben Bacchetti. But he certainly wasn't going to tell her that.

"Nothing solid yet. Why?"

"Billy Barnett would like to take you to dinner. To thank you for the other night."

"Why does everyone want to buy me a meal?"

Stacy shrugged. "It's a Hollywood thing."

Matthew pretended to act amused, but how he truly felt was annoyed. Having lunch the previous day with Ben had been torture enough. The last thing he wanted to do was sit through another meal with a guy he could care less about, especially now that he didn't need access to Billy to get close to Tessa.

"Please tell Mr. Barnett it's not necessary. Besides, he already thanked me."

"Nonsense. What you did was very brave. And he's already on his way to pick you up, so you can't say no. Oh, he also wanted me to mention that Tessa and Ben will be joining you."

Matthew perked up. "Really?"

"Really."

He glanced at Tessa, who was getting in position to shoot again. He figured the scene must be her last of the day. Even so, that meant she wouldn't be getting out of here for another thirty minutes, at the earliest. He'd probably have to sit through a drink alone with Billy, but he could manage doing so knowing that dinner with Tessa would follow.

Her last dinner as Ben's wife.

He caught himself before he started grinning at the thought.

"Well, if I can't say no, then I can't say no."

Stacy smiled. "He said he'll pick you up on the street where the makeup trailers are. You should probably head over there now. He'll be here soon."

Matthew hopped out of his chair. "Sorry, Mr. Chase. You'll have to tell me the rest of your story later."

"Matthew, please. For the thousandth time, call me Logan."

"Right. Sorry, Logan."

"No worries, my friend. The end of the story can wait until next time."

Matthew donned a less than believable smile. "Can't wait."

49

ON HIS WAY TO THE SET, TEDDY MADE A STOP AT THE Santa Barbara Hills Hotel, where he picked up some items from his room and traded the production car he'd been driving for his Porsche.

If things went sideways in his attempt to rescue Rebecca, he preferred to have the speed and agility of his roadster available to him over the clunky handling of the production sedan. Of course, that would still leave him with the Matthew problem. For that, he would need more help than just a fast car.

Once he was back on the road, he called Daniel Rivera and explained what he needed.

"Got it," Rivera said. "I'll make it happen."

"When I get to the set, I'll stall for as long as

I can to give you a head start. Who will be in charge in your absence?"

"Kyle Hansen."

"I have something for him to do, too. Let him know I'll talk to him when I get there."

"Will do."

Teddy arrived at that day's filming location five minutes later. The guards let him through the roadblock, and he parked near the makeup trailers. As instructed, Matthew was waiting there for him.

When Teddy climbed out of his Porsche, Matthew took a step toward him. "You really don't have to do this, Mr. Barnett. It wasn't that big of a deal."

"Not a big deal? Tell that to the bruise on your face."

Matthew touched his cheek, surprised. Apparently, he hadn't realized some of his bruise was showing through the makeup he'd put on.

"You're lucky you weren't more seriously injured," Teddy said. "As far as I'm concerned, dinner is not nearly enough to thank you for what you did."

"I don't know about that."

"I do." Teddy patted Matthew's arm. "I need a quick word with Peter first. You don't mind waiting here for me, do you?"

"Not at all."

Teddy headed to the set. Peter was at his usual spot near the camera, chatting with his father.

Teddy traded greetings with both of them, then said to Peter, "I hear you're running a little behind today."

Peter feigned surprise. "I knew it. You **do** have a spy on the set."

"I do. She's called my assistant, and she's supposed to keep me informed on everything that goes on here. That's how movies get made."

"Ah. So that's how. All these years, I've been thinking it had something to do with cameras and microphones and actors and, well, directors."

"Don't say that too loudly, or the press might find out. I can see the headline now. 'Academy Award–Winning Director Doesn't Know Anything About the Business.'"

"Good point. Probably wouldn't be great for my career."

"Probably not. Do you mind if I borrow your father for a moment?"

"He's all yours."

Teddy and Stone moved to a quiet area, away from the cast and crew.

"Can you go to the Novaks' estate?"

"Now?"

"Yes. Another video should be arriving at seven minutes after six. I'd like you to be there when it does. More specifically, I need you to keep Carl from doing something stupid, like calling the FBI."

"I can do that. But he'll probably ask me how close you are to getting Rebecca back."

"I don't want to overpromise, but between you and me, very."

"So, in other words, stop him from flying off the handle while simultaneously keeping him in the dark."

"You should stop listening to those people who say you don't have a way with words."

Stone headed for the parking area, and Teddy went in search of Kyle Hansen. He found him near the craft services area, grabbing a cup of coffee.

"Mr. Hansen, I'm Billy Barnett, the film's producer." Though Teddy had met Hansen when they'd searched the Novaks' house, it had been in the guise of George Samuels.

Hansen set his cup down and held out a hand. "Mr. Barnett, it's a pleasure to meet you." They shook. "Daniel Rivera told me you need my help with something?"

"I do." Teddy motioned for Hansen to follow him, and then led the acting head of security behind a grip truck, out of sight of everyone. "How do you feel about breaking into a car?"

"I'm generally against it."

"I thought as much. Hold on." Teddy called

Mike Freeman and put him on speaker. "Mike, it's Billy Barnett. I'm here with one of your men." He glanced at Hansen. "It's Kyle, right?"

"Yes, sir."

"His name's Kyle Hansen. I need him to break into Matthew Wagner's car, but I think he'll feel better about it if you gave him the okay."

"Kyle?"

"Yes, Mr. Freeman," Hansen said.

"I not only give you my permission, but you should consider this an assignment straight from me. If there are any repercussions, I will take full responsibility for your actions."

"I understand. If you say it's necessary, then it's necessary."

"It is."

"Thanks, Mike," Teddy said, then hung up.

"What am I looking for?" Hansen asked.

"I'm not exactly sure. Weapons, drugs, anything unusual. I'm taking Matthew away from the set for a while, so don't do anything until we leave."

"Got it."

"When you finish, call me."

Teddy checked his watch on his walk back to his car. He'd been at the set for almost fifteen minutes. That should have been more than enough time for Rivera and the men he'd taken with him to get to where they needed to be.

Matthew was leaning against a telephone pole

near the Porsche when Teddy returned. As soon as he saw Teddy, he stood.

Teddy gave him a wave. "Sorry to keep you waiting. That's the movie business. Every time you say one minute, you mean a quarter hour."

"No problem, Mr. Barnett." While there was a smile on Matthew's face when he said this, Teddy sensed an undercurrent of nervous tension.

They climbed into the car and Teddy drove them away from the set.

"Have you enjoyed your time hanging out with the cast?" Teddy asked.

"Yes, very much. It's been amazing. I never expected to have this kind of opportunity."

"Good thing you had some free time."

"I'm actually here on vacation."

"Oh. You're not from Santa Barbara?"

"No. I live in L.A."

"Is that right? Then it's our good fortune you're here this week. You've helped us out twice."

"Just luck, I guess."

"I believe we make our own luck, Matthew." Teddy glanced over. "This is all happening because of your actions."

"Right place, right time. That's all."

That sounded good, but Teddy caught the brief flicker of concern that crossed Matthew's face, as if he was wondering if Teddy knew something he shouldn't.

If Teddy hadn't already been convinced

that the shooting in which Matthew had come to Stacy and Adriene's aid had somehow been Matthew's doing, he would be now.

As much as Teddy would have liked to take Matthew somewhere he could interrogate him about his true intentions, Teddy needed to be in position when the next hostage video arrived. If he wasn't, he'd lose his only potential chance to locate Rebecca. His chat with Matthew would have to wait. For now, keeping Matthew isolated so he couldn't harm anyone would have to suffice.

Teddy drove them across the city to the edge of the industrial area from where the calls to Kordo had come.

After parking at the curb, he said, "Wait here."

"Where are you going?"

"To take care of a problem for a friend." Teddy climbed out. "Don't worry. I shouldn't be too long."

He opened the Porsche's front trunk, removed his small duffel bag, and disappeared into the space between two buildings.

50

"I'M SORRY," STACY SAID. "I DON'T KNOW WHAT kind of car Matthew drives. Why? Is there a problem?"

Hansen shook his head. "No problem. There are a few cars parked near one of the trucks, and I need to get them moved. I thought one might be his. I would have asked him, but I heard he left."

"He went to dinner with Billy. I mean, Mr. Barnett. I could call him, if you'd like."

"I don't think that's necessary. If it turns out one of the vehicles is his, we can call him then."

Hansen had seen Stacy hanging out with Matthew earlier and had hoped she would have been able to point him in the right direction. So much for the easy route.

He checked with the security guards watching

the lot where the cast and crew had parked, but Matthew hadn't left his car there.

Prior to the recent arrival of reinforcements from Strategic Services, security for **Storm's Eye** had concentrated only on the immediate area where the crew was filming. Now there were enough officers to expand the coverage to the streets surrounding the location.

Hansen made his way around the perimeter, checking with each security team member he encountered.

"You mean Miss Lange's friend? The one who's visiting the set?" said the third guard he'd come to asked.

"That's the guy."

"Sure. He parked down there, about a block and a half." The guard pointed down the street. "Black sedan. A Honda, I think. It has tinted windows."

"Which side of the street?"

"On the right."

Hansen jogged down the sidewalk until he spotted a black Honda Accord, with every window but the front windshield tinted.

Being reluctant to break into a car didn't mean Hansen didn't know how to do it. A majority of security assignments were big events with hundreds, if not thousands, of people. There were always a few in the crowd who lost their keys or locked them in their vehicles. Hansen and many of his colleagues at the company were trained in the art of opening a car.

After making sure there was no one in the vicinity, Hansen pulled on a pair of gloves and disengaged the lock on the front passenger-side door of the Honda.

After sliding into the seat, he opened the glove compartment. The storage space was surprisingly neat. It contained an inch-thick blue plastic sheath, a tire gauge, a tin of mints, and a black case that looked a bit like a long cigarette holder. Inside the sheath, he found the owner manual, the car's registration, and an insurance card. The name listed on the last two was Matthew Wagner.

It was the case that proved most interesting, however. Inside were a pair of empty syringes and two glass medicine bottles. Both bottles held clear liquid, one bottle fuller than the other.

He took a picture of the case and its contents, then returned everything to the compartment.

A quick scan around the cabin revealed an interior as neat as the glove compartment. The seats, the floor, and the dash were all bare. There wasn't even a discarded scrap of paper or wayward coin to be found.

He checked under the passenger seat, but the space was also clean and empty. He reached across and unlocked the driver's door, then moved around the car and climbed in on that side.

Nothing under the driver's seat, either.

Though the car was at least four years old, it was as if it had been driven off a dealer's lot that morning. Even Hansen, who prided himself on how well he took care of his own vehicles, had never been able to keep a car in such pristine shape.

He released the trunk and walked to the back of the car. The only thing in the entire space was a hard-sided, rectangular case.

He picked it up and opened the lid. Inside was a pair of expensive binoculars.

Hansen's brow furrowed. While it wasn't out of the question for someone to have a pair in their car, it seemed odd that they would be the only item in an otherwise empty trunk.

To be thorough, he lifted the bottom of the trunk to check the area beneath. A spare tire and a jack and nothing else. Everything as it should be.

As he lowered the cover again, it caught on something just before it could settle into place. He raised it a few inches and saw that there was something jammed between the left sidewall and the cover.

He leaned in. The obstruction appeared to be round and about an inch and a half in diameter.

He grabbed the curved edge and jiggled the cover a few times before the disc popped free.

To his surprise, it was a button. Not the kind sewn onto shirts and the like, but the kind with messages on them, which could be attached to a bag or a hat or a jacket.

Printed on one side were the words I LOVE YOU TESSA. Underneath the type was a picture of Tessa Tweed and a guy who looked to be in his twenties. Both were smiling at the camera.

Though Hansen had never talked to Matthew, he had seen him from a distance several times. The guy in the picture was not Matthew. But he **was** familiar.

As Hansen stared absently down the street, trying to place the man's face, something fluttered on the windshield of a car, several vehicles away.

He blinked, then cocked his head, realization dawning on him.

He immediately shut Matthew's trunk and jogged over to the other vehicle, then grabbed the flapping sheet from the windshield.

Printed on it in bold type was MISSING: JUSTIN ROGERS. Above this was a picture of the same smiling man who was on the button with Tessa. In fact, in the picture on the flyer, Justin was wearing the very button Hansen was now holding.

He pulled out his phone.

51

"STOP PACING," PAVEL SAID. "YOU'RE DRIVING me crazy."

Instead of stopping, Neno altered his course toward his colleague, and promptly slapped him on the side of the head.

Pavel jerked. "Ow! What the hell?" Rubbing the spot where he'd been hit, he turned angrily to Neno, looking like he was about to jump up to challenge his much smaller boss.

Neno pinned him to his seat with a glare. "Since when do you think it's okay to talk to me like that?"

Pavel grumbled something under his breath, his nostrils flaring.

"What was that?"

"Nothing."

They stared at each other until Pavel finally looked away.

"Sorry, okay?" Pavel said. "You don't need to be so touchy."

When Neno pulled his hand back as if he were going to strike the useless ingrate again, Pavel flinched. Instead of hitting him, Neno said, "You need to learn to keep your mouth shut."

"All right. All right." When Neno cocked his arm again, Pavel raised his hands in defense and said, "I'm shutting up."

Neno held the pose for another moment before scowling and walking back to the other side of the room.

Pavel had far too much self-confidence for someone with his limited experience, and he acted like the world revolved around him. Neno shouldn't have let the punk get to him, but he was too keyed up.

In another few minutes, it would be time to send today's video. It would be the last before the countdown ran out, twenty-four hours from now. Tomorrow, there would be no video, just an email with directions to where Rebecca's body could be found.

With things finally coming to a head, it was understandable that Neno would be on edge. Add in the fact that it had been more than a day since he'd last heard from Kordo, it was a wonder he hadn't killed Pavel instead of only hitting him.

He looked at his watch: 6:04 p.m. Three minutes to go.

Across the room, Pavel was pointing the remote at the TV and flicking through channels. A scene from an old movie. A commercial. A news report about a car accident. Some kind of sporting event.

The hair on the back of Neno's neck stood on end. "Go back."

Pavel continued rotating through channels, as if he hadn't heard him.

Neno rushed over and yanked the remote out of his hand.

"Hey!" Pavel protested.

"I told you to go back!"

Neno tapped rapidly on the remote, backtracking through the channels until he reached the one with the news report. The first clip he had seen had shown a car upside down on the side of a hill. Now, the vehicle was sitting on the back of a flatbed truck.

Despite the half-crushed roof and other damage, Neno found it instantly familiar. It looked just like the car Kordo had been using. Even the color was the same. At the bottom of the screen was a graphic that read: SINGLE CAR CRASH KILLS ONE.

He turned up the volume.

". . . initial reports of yesterday's accident had stated that the driver of the vehicle had been racing up the road alongside another car, which some witnesses claim to have been a Porsche. But according to the sheriff's office, that was not the case."

The scene switched to a sheriff's officer at a podium, a graphic identifying him as Deputy Richard Evert. "The victim is a male, in his early thirties. We will be withholding his identity until his next of kin has been notified. There was no one else in the vehicle, nor were there any other vehicles involved. The driver appears to have lost control of his car when taking a curve at excessive speed. It is a tragic accident, one that could have been a lot worse if other vehicles had been in the vicinity."

Neno's mouth went dry. While there was no way to know for sure that Kordo was the victim, short of calling the police, all of Neno's senses were telling him it was his friend.

The alarm on his phone started ringing. He blinked, confused by the sound. On the screen he saw that it was 6:07, but even then it took a moment before he realized what that meant.

The video.

"Do we have to watch this?" Pavel asked, gesturing at the TV. "It's boring."

Neno considered, then quickly discarded, the idea of telling Pavel what the news report meant. With Kordo now gone, it would only make the punk more likely to question Neno's authority.

Besides, Neno had something much more important to deal with.

He dropped the remote in Pavel's lap and opened his phone's settings. After turning off airplane mode, he went to his email app, where the message with the video was ready to go, and hit SEND.

52

TEN MINUTES EARLIER, TEDDY ROUNDED THE CORNER of the unused building that sat next to where he'd parked his Porsche. As instructed, Rivera was waiting for him there.

"Your men are in position?"

Rivera nodded. "They have eyes on Matthew now. If he moves, we'll know."

"I don't want to scare him, so make sure he doesn't see anyone, unless he tries to leave the area. If he does, stop him."

"Understood." Rivera pulled a set of communications gear from his pocket and held it out to Teddy. "Put it on channel one for everyone, and channel two if you just want to talk to me."

"Thanks."

"You mentioned there was something else we might be able to help you with?"

Teddy raised the hand that held his comm set. "I'll radio if I need you."

"Got it." Rivera headed back to the street.

As soon as he was gone, Teddy exchanged the suit jacket and button-down shirt he'd been wearing for a long-sleeve black T-shirt from the duffel bag. He also removed a pair of gloves and a black ski mask but didn't don either yet.

A check of the time told him it was 6:03 p.m. It shouldn't be long now.

He looped the comm earpiece over his ear, adjusted the mic that protruded from it so that it pointed toward his mouth, and turned it on.

"Test, test. This is Billy Barnett."

A click was followed by Rivera's voice. "Coming in loud and clear, Mr. Barnett."

"Copy."

Teddy's phone began to vibrate with a call. The name on the screen read **KYLE HANSEN**.

"I just finished looking through Matthew's car."

"And?"

"I found a syringe kit in the glove compartment, and a couple bottles of clear liquid. No labels."

"Is that so?"

"I can send you a picture."

"Later. Was there anything else?"

"Yeah." The way Hansen said this, Teddy knew whatever it was bothered the security officer more than the syringes. "Have you seen those flyers people have been handing out the last couple days? The one about the missing person?"

That was not what Teddy had been expecting Hansen to say. "For Justin . . . something?"

"Justin Rogers."

"Right. I have. There was one on my car. Why?"

"I found something in Matthew's trunk that belonged to Rogers. A button that says 'I love you Tessa.'"

"That could belong to anyone. I've seen dozens around the set."

"Not this one. It has a picture in the background of Rogers and Tessa. And it's the same button he's wearing in the photo on the flyer."

Teddy closed his eyes for a moment, trying to recall the flyer. One of the things that had kept him alive in the years during and after his time in the CIA was a combination of an excellent memory and attention to detail. And though he'd only looked at the piece of paper for a few seconds, he could see the photo of Justin in his mind and recalled the unique button.

The coincidence was too obvious to ignore. This wasn't definitive proof of anything, but Teddy had a bad feeling growing in his gut.

An image of the pile of dirt-covered clothes in the bathroom of Matthew's rental flashed in his mind, and Teddy's bad feeling veered toward horrible certainty.

"Make sure no one else touches the car," Teddy said. "The police are going to want to take a look at it."

"Should I call them?"

"Not yet. I'll tell you when. Thanks, Kyle. Good work."

When Teddy hung up, it was 6:06 p.m.

Just a few more seconds, and if everything worked the way Kevin said it should, Teddy would soon know the location of the kidnapper's phone and, hopefully, Rebecca.

When the time clicked over to 6:07 and no alert appeared on his phone, he frowned.

Had Kevin's tracking hack for the other phone not worked? Or had Teddy been wrong about the phone in the first place, and it wasn't the device the kidnappers were using to send the videos?

Teddy stared at the screen, waiting for the minute to change from seven to eight. Even if this failed, it was possible Kevin would find something useful in the internet data. But that could take time, and every moment was precious.

Ten seconds before the clock changed, Teddy's phone pinged and a text window appeared on his screen:

DEVICE LOCATED

53

NENO SHUT THE PHONE COMPLETELY OFF AND TOSSED
it on the table. What he wished he could do was
smash it with a hammer, but he still needed it for
the final message tomorrow.

He wanted this job done. He wanted to fly
back home tonight and never return to America
again. He'd already been antsy before, when
Kordo had simply gone quiet. Now, with Kordo
presumably dead, it felt as if the walls were closing in on him.

He glanced out the door to the hallway.

He could kill the woman now and get the hell
out of there. It wasn't like they were going to let
her go tomorrow. He could take the pictures of
her body and send the final email from anywhere.

Only he couldn't. Not if he valued his own

life. Janic had a plan, and he had been **very** clear that no deviations from it would be tolerated.

"She dies the minute the countdown runs out," Janic had told Neno. "Not a minute before. Not a minute after. I want Novak to suffer like my family suffered. I want him to keep thinking he can save her, that there is something he can do, until it's too late."

Janic had then ordered Neno to provide him with a live feed of her execution. No way Neno could fake that. At least, not without the very real chance of his boss realizing the truth. And if that happened, Kordo wouldn't be the only employee of Janic's who died on this mission.

"It's only one more day," he whispered to himself. Kordo was gone because he was sloppy. But at least he'd died before anyone had gotten to him. "No one knows we're here. It will be fine. Everything will be fine."

Pavel looked over his shoulder. "Did you say something?"

"Huh? No."

With a roll of his eyes, Pavel turned back to the cop show he was watching.

Neno glared at the back of Pavel's head. "It's time to prepare her dinner."

"What does it matter? She'll be dead tomorrow."

"She's not dead yet."

"It can wait until my show is over."

"Pavel!"

"If you're so uptight about it, then you do it."

Neno's cheeks grew hot as his anger started to boil. He was about to order Pavel to get off his ass, but then checked himself.

Maybe he **should** do it. He needed to do something to work off his tension, and hanging around here worrying about every way things could still go wrong would only make things worse.

He warmed a fast-food burger in the microwave, then grabbed a can of soda from the cooler and his mask off the counter, before heading into the hall.

54

TEDDY WAS HALFWAY TO THE LOCATION THAT matched the dot glowing on his map, when a new alert flashed on his screen:

SIGNAL LOST

The phone he was tracking had been turned off again. This only further convinced him that it was the one used to send the email. To verify the timing, he shot off a text to Stone.

Did the video arrive?

Stone replied immediately.

Yes. Just a few seconds ago.

Teddy looked at the map again. Though the phone's signal had been lost, the device's last-known location was still highlighted.

He eased along an overgrown chain-link fence until he could see the building that matched the spot on the map.

It appeared to be an unused, two-story office building, with a large sign in front proclaiming the property for sale. No cars were parked in the attached lot.

The perfect location for a group of kidnappers to set up shop.

Teddy pulled on his mask and gloves, then he sneaked over to the only door along the rear wall.

Most of the concrete that abutted the build-ing was covered by a layer of dust and trash, built up over months of neglect. The exception was the area in front of a single exit door, where the concrete had been swept clean by the door's recent opening and closing. This had to be the right place.

When Teddy leaned close, he could hear a tele-vision inside. The noise was coming from closer to the back door than he would have liked. Better if he could find a more secluded way in.

He crept to the corner and peeked down the side of the building. He'd been hoping to spot something he could use to climb to the roof and sneak in that way. But what he discovered was even better—a set of stairs that descended into an opening in the ground. He hurried over and took them down to a basement door at the bottom.

Again, he listened, but this time he heard nothing on the other side.

After making quick work of the lock, he slipped inside what appeared to be a dark basement hallway. He flipped on his phone's flashlight. Undisturbed dust covered the entire floor, telling him no one had been here in a long time.

He headed down the hall and checked each door he came to until he found a stairwell.

Two voices drifted down from the ground floor. They were muffled but clear enough that he could tell they weren't speaking in English.

As Teddy headed up, he detected an undercurrent of anger in one of the voices. He didn't like that. An agitated kidnapper could quickly turn into a killer.

By the time Teddy reached the first-floor landing, the voices had stopped. He could hear someone moving around and the noise from the TV, but that was it.

He crept out of the stairwell onto the first floor.

PAVEL SNICKERED AT THE TV. THE CRIMINAL IN THE show he was watching was stupid. He should have left town the moment he knew the police were on to him, but instead, he thought he could hide at the apartment of his girlfriend's sister.

Like the cops would never figure that out.

If it were him, Pavel would have either stayed out of town until everything cooled down or gathered his friends and killed the cops giving him problems. Probably the second one. It would be simpler. Not to mention more fun.

These American TV shows were so unrealistic.

Behind him, he heard Neno walk out of the room with the woman's dinner, and he instantly felt more relaxed. Neno was a zero chill, pain in the ass who did not respect Pavel the way he should. Kordo wasn't much better, but at least Kordo mostly ignored him when he was around.

Pavel could hardly wait until he was back home. Mr. Janic owed him big for doing this job. There was no way he would accept crappy assignments like this anymore. He wanted the good stuff. The stuff he could skim a little off the top from and show people who's boss.

On the TV, cops in protective gear were gathered in front of the apartment door, ready to burst in.

Pavel chuckled again and turned up the volume.

55

MOMENTS BEFORE, TEDDY MADE HIS WAY DOWN THE short hallway to where it intersected with another and checked around the corner. At the far end, a man was walking in the opposite direction, carrying a soda can and something wrapped in paper.

While there were several doors between him and Teddy, only one was open, and out of it drifted the sound of the TV.

The man in the hallway turned right and disappeared down another corridor. Teddy eased around the corner, his gun leading the way, and crept to the open door.

The only person in the room was a man sitting on a wooden chair, facing the television that was the source of all the noise. The guy had his legs stretched out, and every few seconds, he pushed on his heels, raising the front legs of the chair off the floor.

Teddy entered the room and stepped lightly across the space until he was behind the man.

The cop show on the TV was a rerun Teddy had seen. In mere seconds, the cops were going to raid an apartment, and things were going to get very noisy.

The moment the battering ram hit the apartment door and the cops began yelling, Teddy yanked back on the man's already off-balance chair and sent it crashing to the floor.

Before the kidnapper could do anything more than flail his arms, Teddy stepped on his throat and pointed his gun at the middle of the man's face.

"Hi there."

The man grabbed Teddy's leg. But when Teddy wagged his gun at him, he reluctantly let go.

"Speak English?"

The man responded with a glare, so Teddy ground his foot into the guy's Adam's apple. Out of desperation, the kidnapper grabbed Teddy's leg again and tried to push it off, but immediately let go when Teddy jammed the business end of his silencer into the guy's forehead.

"English. Yes or no?"

"Yes," the guy croaked. "A little."

"Where are you keeping her?"

The man's eyes flared in surprise, then turned guarded. "Keeping who?"

"Nice try, buddy. I've already killed your friend Kordo, and if you don't want to help me, I don't mind getting a little more blood on my hands."

"Kordo? Kordo's dead?"

The man's response confirmed what Teddy had already hoped to be true: he was definitely in the right place.

"I guess news is a little slow getting around. Now, where is she?"

The guy tried to swallow, which was near impossible under the circumstances.

"If you're not going to talk, I guess I have no choice." Teddy lifted his gun and moved his aim from the man's head to his chest.

"She is . . . she is upstairs. Room in center of . . . building."

"See, that wasn't so hard. She **is** still alive, isn't she?"

"Yes, yes! Still alive. Neno just take her dinner."

"Neno? That's your friend who just walked out of here."

"Yes."

"How many more of you are there?"

"What?"

"You, Neno, Kordo. How many more?"

The man glanced away and then back. "Ten."

"If you're going to lie, then I have no use for you."

Teddy's finger moved along the trigger, as if it was about to pull it.

"Wait," the man squeaked. "No more. Only me and Neno here."

From the look in the man's eyes, Teddy could tell this was the truth.

"Thank you. One more question. When were you planning on killing Rebecca?"

The man blinked. "Killing? No, we . . . we letting her go. Tomorrow. Letting her go tomorrow. Yes. No killing."

"And you were doing so well," Teddy said, knowing **this** was a lie.

He squeezed the trigger.

56

"JUST A LITTLE MORE," REBECCA GRUNTED UNDER her breath.

She was lying on the floor, half beneath her cot, trying to loosen one of the bolts holding the bed together.

She needed something she could use as a weapon. Unfortunately, the only things she had to work with were the cot and the small plastic table. The latter was basically worthless. Even if she could break off one of its legs, it wouldn't be strong enough to do more than annoy whoever she hit with it.

The cot's legs were metal, however, so she had concentrated her effort on freeing one. But when one bolt after another wouldn't budge, she'd decided that if she could get a single bolt undone, the small piece of metal would be better than nothing.

Her persistence paid off, and now the seventh bolt she'd tried was just a rotation or two from being free.

Footsteps echoed in the hallway, on the other side of the door.

"No, no, no, no, no," she whispered, turning the bolt faster.

As she heard a key enter the lock, the bolt fell from its hole. She scrambled to catch it before it clattered to the floor. The instant her fingers wrapped around it, she scooted out from under the bed, and was sitting on the mattress a heartbeat before the door opened.

Like always, the man who entered wore a white plastic mask over his face. Surprisingly, he appeared to be alone, though. That was a first.

"Stay on the bed," he said.

"Not going anywhere."

"And shut up."

"Sorry," she said, her tone meek and unthreatening.

As he carried a soda can and what was probably a hamburger toward the table, she tightened her hand around the bolt and glanced at the open door. She was sure she couldn't be this lucky, and that one of his asshole buddies would show themselves at any moment. But none did.

She shifted the bolt so that the long threaded

end stuck out between her index and ring fingers. The moment the man's back was partially to her, she launched herself at him, aiming the bolt at the nearest eyehole in his mask.

Her kidnapper turned in surprise just quickly enough so that her makeshift weapon slammed into the nose of his mask, instead of the eyehole. The plastic cracked and tore into his skin. The man jerked away from her, causing the bolt to scrape sideways into the eyehole and rip across his cornea.

He stumbled away, screaming.

Not waiting to see what he did next, Rebecca raced out the door.

NENO BLINKED, BUT THAT ONLY MADE THE PAIN worse.

"You bitch!" he yelled.

He ripped the mask off and forced himself to stand. This rerouted the blood pouring from the gash on his nose to run into his mouth. He coughed, then wiped the flow away and looked around through his undamaged eye, planning to beat the crap out of Rebecca.

Only she wasn't there.

He turned to the doorway.

The **open** doorway.

"Dammit!"

He rushed after her.

AS TEDDY REACHED THE SECOND-FLOOR LANDING, HE heard a man shout in pain. It had come from somewhere on the same floor, but distant.

Keeping as quiet as possible, he ran toward the noise.

A second, angrier yell echoed into the hallway just as Teddy reached an intersection of corridors. Then he heard someone running.

Pressing himself against the wall, Teddy peered around the corner. He caught momentary sight of Neno sprinting away from him, then disappearing into another hallway.

Teddy ran after him, not slowing until he passed an open door about halfway down the hall. Glancing inside, he immediately recognized the space as the room where the videos of Rebecca had been recorded. No one was there now, though.

When Teddy had seen Neno a few seconds ago, the kidnapper had clearly been alone, alone and angry. That had to mean Rebecca was trying to escape.

Teddy sped down the hall.

57

"THERE'S NO WAY OUT!"

Rebecca glanced over her shoulder. Her captor hadn't found her yet, but from his shouts, she knew he was getting close.

The building was a maddening maze of corridors, with no apparent exits. Every time she passed an open doorway, she glanced in, hoping to find a door to the outside or at least someplace she could hide. But so far, there had been neither.

Ahead, several boxes were piled against the corridor wall, and just beyond them was the start of another hallway leading off to the left.

"Stop!" the man yelled, his voice suddenly much louder.

She glanced back again and could now see him sprinting toward her. His mask was gone, and blood covered part of his face, but not enough to hide his rage.

Terrified, she increased her speed. As she passed the boxes, she yanked on one in the middle. The stack teetered, then crashed onto the floor a second after she went by. It wouldn't stop him, but it should slow him down a step or two.

She raced into the new corridor, and nearly skidded to a halt. Twenty feet down, the hall dead-ended. A pair of doors were just before it, one on the right and one on the left.

She hurried to them, praying one would be a way out. But each only led to an empty room.

She ducked into the one on the left and pressed against the wall next to the door. As quietly as she could, she moved through the darkness toward the far corner.

Halfway there, she gasped and jerked her foot back. It had knocked against something on the floor. Her first thought was a rat, but when she heard no skittering of feet, she poked the spot with her toe.

Whatever it was, it was solid but not connected to the floor.

She reached down.

TEDDY TURNED THE CORNER IN TIME TO SEE NENO hop over a pile of boxes near the other end of the hall. He raised his gun, but before he could get a shot off, Neno vanished into a corridor on the left.

NENO CAME TO A FULL STOP WHEN HE ENTERED THE dead-end hallway. Though the woman was nowhere in sight, there were only two places she could be.

He walked toward the two doorways, a sneer creasing his face.

Which room would she have chosen? The right? Or the left?

He turned on his flashlight and shone it into the one on the right. The space was empty.

As he turned his beam to check the room on the left, it lit up Rebecca, standing right behind him. Her hands were wrapped around a two-foot-long piece of wood that was swinging toward his head.

He threw up an arm, and the club smashed into it so hard one of his bones snapped with an audible **crack.**

She tried to get around him as he screamed in agony. He thrust out his good arm just in time to grab her by the hair and yank her back. She fought to pull free, so he kicked her feet out from under her, and sent her plunging to the floor.

To hell with what Janic wants. This ends tonight.

He reached for the gun in his shoulder holster.

TEDDY LEAPT OVER THE BOXES AND DASHED INTO THE new hallway. Rebecca lay on the floor, with Neno glaring down at her.

As the kidnapper reached for his weapon, Teddy jerked his own up and pulled the trigger. His bullet smashed into Neno's shoulder, spinning him into the wall at the end of the corridor and sending his gun tumbling out of his grasp.

Neno pressed his back against the wall and kept on his feet. When he spotted Teddy, a brief flash of confusion clouded his face before fury washed it away. He scanned the floor until his eyes found his weapon.

Teddy took two steps toward him. "Not a good idea. Unless you enjoy getting shot. In which case, go for it."

Neno deflated, as if admitting defeat, then lunged for the gun.

Teddy hadn't been fooled, and by the time Neno's fingers wrapped around the pistol, Teddy was towering above him. He stomped on the weapon, smashing Neno's fingers between metal and floor.

"I did warn you," Teddy said.

Neno screamed. "Go ahead, then. Kill me."

"Why the rush? There'll be plenty of time for that later."

Teddy smashed his silencer into the man's temple, bouncing Neno's head off the floor and knocking the kidnapper unconscious.

Teddy turned to Rebecca. She had pushed up against the wall and was looking warily at him.

"Who are you?"

"Me? I'm nobody. But you're Rebecca Novak, and you have one very worried husband waiting for you at home."

"Carl sent you?"

"That he did." He held out a hand to her. "Let me help you up."

58

MATTHEW LOOKED DOWN THE STREET AT THE GAP between buildings into which Billy had disappeared. That had been over ten minutes ago.

He didn't like this. Something felt . . . wrong.

The place the Porsche was parked next to looked deserted, as did a few other buildings in the area. And though several cars were parked along the street, he hadn't seen a soul since Billy left.

Billy had said he was taking care of something for a friend, but what did that mean? And why park here, when he could have parked closer to whatever he had to do?

It didn't make any sense.

Matthew had already been on edge from Billy's earlier comment.

This is all happening because of your actions.

He knew Billy meant it as a compliment, but it had hit a little too close to the truth for Matthew's liking.

He looked down the street again and cursed under his breath. If he sat there a second longer, he was going to go crazy. He threw open the door and stepped onto the sidewalk, hoping that stretching his legs would calm him down.

It did not.

Maybe if he saw where Billy had gone, he'd feel better. Newly determined, he started walking toward the building gap the producer had entered.

He made it three steps when the sound of a car door opening ahead of him echoed down the street. A half block up, a man climbed out of a sedan and stopped on the sidewalk, facing Matthew.

The early-evening gloom turned the guy into more of a silhouette than an actual person, but Matthew could see enough to tell the man was tall and broad-shouldered.

Another door opened, this one coming from behind.

Matthew turned and saw another large man standing on the sidewalk, looking his way.

Matthew's panic skyrocketed right through antsy to full-on freaking out. No vehicles had driven by since he and Billy arrived. These men must have been parked there the whole time.

He had no idea what they could possibly want, but whatever it was, he didn't want to stick around to find out.

He needed to get out of there.

Fast.

Unfortunately, the Porsche wasn't an option, as Billy had taken its keys with him. So any escape would have to be on foot.

After a quick glance at the men watching him, he strode toward the front of Billy's car, intent on crossing the street and losing himself among the buildings on the other side.

But before he could set a foot on the asphalt, yet another car door opened. This one was on the opposite side of the road, a couple of car lengths back.

A third man stepped out. "Mr. Wagner. Billy Barnett would appreciate it if you remained in his vehicle until he returns."

Matthew froze. This man was close enough that the evening shadows didn't obscure his face. Matthew had seen him earlier, on the set of **Storm's Eye.** He was one of the security officers. Which meant the other two must be the same.

Why would Billy have people watching him?

Unless what Billy had said hadn't been a compliment after all. That he'd meant it exactly the way Matthew feared.

No, that's not possible.

There was no way Billy could know about Matthew's plans.

Could he?

This is all happening because of your actions.

Oh, crap.

Matthew had been discovered. It was the only logical conclusion. And if that was true, he was in a load of trouble.

He could remain here and attempt to fabricate a feasible lie to deter Billy's thinking. But time was short and if he failed to come up with something believable, he'd lose any chance he had of being with Tessa. And that was out of the question.

What he had to do was get away from these assholes. Now. After that, he could come up with another plan. If it took him a few more months or even years, it didn't matter. Tessa would be his.

Their destiny was to be together.

He turned back to the sidewalk, acting like he was doing as he'd been told.

While he'd been waiting in the car earlier, he'd noticed several busted windows on the second floor of the building next to the Porsche. Now he covertly scanned the building's façade, and spotted a pipe running up the wall and an old metal awning over the first-floor entrance. He could climb the former to the latter, then duck inside. It wasn't a perfect solution to his problem, but it would do for a start.

He took one more step, and then sprinted toward the pipe.

59

"ARE YOU HURT?" TEDDY ASKED REBECCA, AS HE checked her for obvious injuries.

"No, I'm okay." She looked down the hallway, still tense. "There are at least two others. We need to—"

"Not anymore."

She turned back to him, her brow furrowing. "Are you sure?"

"I've never been surer of anything."

She visibly relaxed.

"Will you be all right here alone for a few moments?" he asked.

"Where are you going?"

Teddy nodded toward Neno's unmoving form. "I want to make sure our friend doesn't try to go anywhere when he wakes up."

"Of course."

Teddy dragged Neno into one of the rooms at the end of the hall. Janic's man had a broken arm, several broken fingers, one eye swollen shut, and a ragged wound on his nose that was leaking blood over his face. Though his breathing was raspy and wet, it wasn't in danger of stopping any time soon.

Teddy pulled the man's arms behind his back, and the unconscious man groaned in pain.

Teddy extracted several zip ties from his pocket. "If you didn't like that, you're **really** not going to like this."

He bound Neno's wrists together first, his ankles second, and then secured them to each other, hog-tying him. Even if Neno hadn't been injured, he wouldn't be going anywhere.

As Teddy stood up, the radio in his ear beeped twice. "Daniel Rivera for Mr. Barnett."

Teddy activated his mic. "Go for Barnett."

"Sir, we have a problem."

"What is it?"

"Matthew tried to make a run for it."

"Tried?"

"He's hiding in a building near where you parked. We have it surrounded, so he's not going anywhere. Do you want us to move in and capture him?"

"No. I'll deal with him. Just make sure he knows your people are outside, so he doesn't do anything stupid. Or, I guess, stupider."

"Copy."

"Daniel, I could use your help here. Can your men handle things there without you?"

"They can. Where are you?"

MATTHEW PRESSED HIMSELF AGAINST THE WALL, next to the third-floor window, and leaned over just enough to see outside.

A parking area stretched out to a chain-link fence, its surface veined by weed-filled cracks. Standing in the otherwise empty lot were two security men, one almost directly below Matthew and the other at the other end of the building.

He rolled back out of sight. "Dammit."

He'd checked the other three sides already, and they were covered, too.

No chance he'd be able to get out unseen. His only choice was to find someplace in the building where he could hide and wait them out.

He'd already searched the third floor and the two below and found nothing, so he went up to the fourth. It turned out to be even more unsuitable than the others, as it was a mostly open space where he'd be spotted in a second.

On the fifth floor, he found a loose panel that gave him access into the space between walls. It might work in a pinch, but the idea of closing himself into such a confined spot was not appealing.

He took the stairs up one more flight and exited onto the roof. It only took a quick look around to know that the top of the building had nowhere to hide, either.

Another curse was forming in his mouth when an idea hit him.

He hurried to the south end of the building, looked over the side, and grimaced. While the gap between his building and the one next door was narrow enough to leap across, the other structure was only two stories high. If a drop that far didn't kill him, it would surely break more than just his legs.

He jogged to the north end. Below was the alleyway that Billy had disappeared into earlier. Standing in it now and keeping an eye on the first floor was another of the film production's security men.

Here the next-door structure was a little bit farther away than the one on the south side, but it was four stories high. If Matthew could get up enough speed and push off at the right moment, he was sure he could easily make the jump. Once he was on the other building, he could quietly sneak out, without the men waiting below knowing.

He nodded to himself, took a deep breath, and began pacing away from the edge.

When he reached the point where he thought he'd have enough of a running start, he swiveled back toward his target. He imagined himself running across the roof, planting his foot on the edge, and launching himself into the air.

"You can do this," he whispered. "For Tessa. Just keep your knees loose and be ready to roll."

As he adjusted his stance so he could get a good push when he started, the roof access door opened.

Matthew looked back, assuming one of the security men had followed him up, but it was Billy Barnett. Only instead of the suit jacket and button-down shirt he'd had on before, Billy was wearing a long-sleeve black T-shirt.

The producer walked toward him, his hands behind his back. "Hello, Matthew. What are you doing up here?"

"Why did you have people watching me?"

"It's a dangerous neighborhood. Didn't want you to accidentally get into trouble."

There was still the very small possibility Billy didn't know the truth, and Matthew could salvage the situation. Playing the wronged man, he grimaced and said, "Right. That's why they're acting like I'm a criminal. But I haven't done anything wrong."

"We both know that's not true."

Billy moved his hands out from behind his back and held up two bags. Two bags that looked exactly like the ones Matthew had left on the roof of the Santa Barbara Hills Hotel.

Matthew tried to play them off with a shrug and a shake of his head. "What are those?"

"We've been to your apartment in L.A., Matthew. And in the room you've been renting here. We've seen the pictures. We know what you've been up to. We know about your feelings for Tessa. As for these?" Billy glanced at the bundles. "My guess is you planned to use them to get rid of Ben. Am I close?"

"That . . . that's ridiculous."

Billy took a few more steps toward Matthew. "Is it? Then perhaps you'd rather talk about what happened to Justin Rogers."

Matthew's eyes widened and his mouth went dry.

How could anyone, let alone Billy Barnett, know about Justin? No one had seen what happened. Matthew was positive of that. And not a soul had been within miles of him when he'd buried the pain in the ass's body in the mountains.

In a less than steady voice, he said, "I don't know who you're talking about."

"I think you do."

When Billy took another step forward, Matthew stepped back and blurted out, "Don't come any closer!"

"It's over, Matthew. You know you can't get away, so there's no need to make a scene. Things will go easier for you if you cooperate. How about you and I go downstairs?"

When Billy shifted his weight like he was going to take another step, Matthew yelled, "I said no closer!"

"Okay. No closer. Then you come to me."

Matthew stared at Billy without seeing him.

This couldn't be happening. There was no way Matthew's dream was over. Not like this. Billy didn't have the right to decide that. The only one who could was Matthew, and he for damn sure wasn't ready to throw in the towel.

There had to be a way to salvage his plans. A way that he and Tessa could be together without interference from loathsome meddlers like Billy Barnett. All Matthew needed was time to figure things out.

He glanced over his shoulder at the building gap. He was a little closer to it than he'd intended, but not enough that it should make a difference.

He turned back to Billy, his confidence returning. "Nothing's over until **I** say it's over. I have a destiny, and you're only a bump in my road to it. If I need to get rid of you, too, I will." He smirked. "I advise you to watch your back, Mr. Barnett."

With that, Matthew spun around and sprinted toward the edge of the roof.

◆ ◆ ◆

"MATTHEW, NO!"

Teddy raced after Matthew. But while he was fast, Matthew had legs that were younger and faster. Teddy was still several yards back when Matthew launched himself over the gap.

As Matthew dropped out of sight, Teddy slowed and then stopped at the edge.

Matthew must have thought the roof of the neighboring building was closer than it was, because instead of landing on it, his body was now sprawled on the ground, five stories below.

60

"IT'S OVER," TEDDY SAID INTO HIS PHONE. HE WAS wearing his dress shirt and jacket again, looking nothing like the masked man from earlier.

"You found Rebecca?" Stone asked.

"Yes."

"Is she—"

"She's okay. Shaken but otherwise unharmed."

"That's great news. I'll let Novak know. You're bringing her here?"

"Yes. We'll be on our way in a few minutes. When we get there, there's something I need you to do."

After telling Stone what he wanted, Teddy went in search of Rivera, and found him standing beside the sedan in which Rebecca sat.

"You're clear on your instructions?"

Rivera nodded. "All set."

Once Teddy and Rebecca left, Rivera would call the police, and feed them the story Teddy had come up with.

Teddy had kept it simple. Matthew had been acting suspicious on set, so Rivera had followed him here. Matthew had seen him, become spooked, and disappeared into the building. He'd jumped to his death before Rivera could find him again.

There would be no mention of Rebecca Novak, the kidnapping, or the nearby building where she'd been held. When the police later searched Matthew's car, they would find Justin's button, which Hansen was, at that very moment, returning to where he'd found it.

Teddy opened the back door of the sedan. "Mrs. Novak, I'm Billy Barnett, an associate of your husband's. If you come with me, I'll take you home."

CARL NOVAK, MORI, AND STONE WERE WAITING outside the Novaks' mansion when Teddy and Rebecca arrived in Teddy's Porsche. Rebecca's husband rushed over before Teddy had even stopped the car.

Novak helped his wife out and they fell into

each other's arms. As Teddy had requested, Stone recorded video of the entire scene on his phone.

Ten minutes later, they were all in the Novaks' living room. Rebecca sat next to her husband, leaning on his shoulder. Novak had asked her if she wanted to go to their room to sleep, but even though she was clearly tired, she insisted on staying.

"I can't thank you enough," Novak said to Teddy.

"**We** can't thank you enough," Rebecca corrected him.

"You're right. **We** can't." Novak smiled at his wife before looking back at Teddy. "I should have never doubted you or your friend."

"You trusted us enough to let us do what needed to be done. That's what's important." Teddy paused, then said, "There's something my friend asked me to pass on."

"Yes?" Novak said.

"He thinks it would be in everyone's best interest if you kept what happened to Mrs. Novak to yourselves."

"No worries there. We have no intentions of letting anyone know."

"Perfect." Teddy looked at Rebecca. "He also said it would help him if you were to avoid being seen in public for the next twenty-four hours. In fact, he said it would be best if you stayed in the house."

"That shouldn't be a problem," Rebecca said, her eyelids heavy. "I have no plans to get out of bed for at least that long."

"Can we ask why?" Novak said.

"There are a few loose ends he needs to tie up. Nothing you need worry about."

Novak looked curious but didn't ask anything more.

Teddy and Stone left not long after. Before getting into their respective vehicles, Teddy gave Stone a quick recap of the evening's events.

"What are you going to do with the kidnapper?" Stone asked.

"I'm going to have a talk with him."

"And then?"

"And then I'll need to borrow your jet."

61

JANIC CHECKED THE CLOCK ON HIS COMPUTER SCREEN again and smiled.

The culmination of his long-awaited revenge was finally here.

While it was the middle of the night in Croatia, in Santa Barbara, California, it was nearing 6:07 p.m. At long last, Neno and his crew would end Rebecca Novak's life and deliver Carl Novak the final blow of the payback he so richly deserved.

Janic's computer dinged with an incoming email. It was from Neno and contained the expected link. When Janic clicked on it, a video window appeared that was currently filled with black. Any second now, Neno would activate the live feed that would let Janic witness the woman's execution.

There had been no way he would miss it.

At six minutes after the hour, an image of Rebecca's cell replaced the black screen. Only the woman wasn't there.

Neno must be preparing her, Janic thought. He'd better hurry, though. Janic had been **very** clear on the timing. And if Neno screwed it up, Janic would not be pleased.

He grew more and more unsettled as the seconds passed without the woman appearing.

"Where is she?" he growled.

Then, right as the clock ticked over to seven minutes after the hour, the image changed again.

Janic's brow furrowed. "What the hell is this?"

The shot started out as a blur of motion, slowing just enough for Janic to get the impression of bricks or cobblestones. When it tilted up, it revealed Carl Novak running to a sports car that was pulling to a stop on a cobblestoned road or driveway. Novak yanked the door open and helped a woman out of the passenger seat.

Janic stared in shock as they embraced each other. The woman was Rebecca Novak.

This had to be a mistake. The footage must have been from Neno's stakeouts before the kidnapping.

Except the framing was too close and steady

to have been taken from a distance. And now that he'd had a good look at Novak's wife, Janic was sure she was wearing the same clothes she'd had on in the videos Neno sent to her husband.

And then Carl Novak spoke, and Janic felt like his head was going to explode. "Are you all right? Did they hurt you?"

"I'm okay," Rebecca replied. "Just . . . tired."

"I've been so worried. I thought I might never see you again."

He pulled her into another hug.

This video wasn't from before the kidnapping. Somehow Rebecca had escaped.

Janic's hand shook with rage as he reached for his phone to call Neno.

When his fingers wrapped around the receiver, something pricked the back of his neck. He tried to jerk his head around to see what it was, but he couldn't move it.

He couldn't move anything.

Unhurried footsteps circled from behind him, and a man stepped into view.

"Hello, Mr. Janic," Teddy Fay said.

TEDDY WAITED UNTIL THE JET WAS IN THE AIR BEFORE he called Stone.

"How was the trip?" Stone asked.

"Fast but fruitful." The prearranged phrase let

Stone know that the Novaks no longer needed to worry about Zoran Janic.

"Glad to hear it. Good timing, too. The Novaks asked me to convey their thanks again."

"You saw them today? They should be lying low."

"They asked Ben and me to come by this afternoon. The final documents haven't been signed yet, but I can tell you that the Novaks have chosen Centurion Studios as their production partner."

"That's fantastic news."

"We'll celebrate when you get back."

Teddy pushed the button that started the process of changing his seat into a lay-flat bed. "I look forward to it."

"Oh. And, Teddy?"

"Yes?"

"Peter says he needs Mark back on the set tomorrow morning."

"I'm sorry, Stone. What was that? There seems to be a connection problem. Can you repeat—"

Teddy hit DISCONNECT, then turned his phone off and closed his eyes.

ABOUT THE AUTHORS

STUART WOODS was the author of more than ninety novels, including the #1 **New York Times** bestselling Stone Barrington series. A native of Georgia and an avid sailor and pilot, he began his writing career in the advertising industry. **Chiefs,** his debut in 1981, won the Edgar Award. Woods passed away in 2022.

STUARTWOODS.COM
Facebook: STUARTWOODSAUTHOR

BRETT BATTLES is the New York Times best-selling author of more than forty novels, including the Jonathan Quinn, Rewinder, Project Eden, and Night Man Chronicles series. He is a three-time Barry Award nominee, winning for Best Thriller in 2009 for his novel **The Deceived.**

BRETTBATTLES.COM
Twitter: BRETTBATTLES

LIKE WHAT YOU'VE READ?

Try these titles by Stuart Woods,
also available in large print:

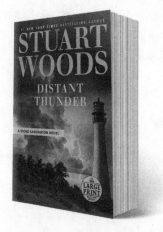

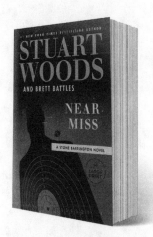

Distant Thunder
ISBN 978-0-593-63261-1

Near Miss
ISBN 978-0-593-63262-8

Black Dog
ISBN 978-0-593-61374-0

For more information on large print titles, visit
www.penguinrandomhouse.com/large-print-format-books